Billia

By
Cassandra Ulrich

To. Jennifer,

You Got Game ?

Cassandra Ulrich

Billiard Buddies

By Cassandra Ulrich

Copyright © Cassandra Ulrich, 2014

Edited by Patti Brock
pattilbrock@yahoo.com

Cover art by Elisa Elaine Luevanos
www.ladymaverick81.com

Cover art Cassandra Ulrich © 2019

Published by: Cassandra Ulrich
P.O. Box 492
Collingswood, NJ 08108-0492
Email: cassandra@cassandraulrich.com

Visit http://cassandraulrich.com/

10 9 8 7 6 5 4 3 2

Printed in The United States of America

Dedication

To Dad who taught me to appreciate the game of pool and gifted me with a cool cue stick.

To Jessica

Acknowledgements

Ernest Ulrich – Thank you for inspiring all my love stories.

My boys and Danielle, my reading buddy – Thanks for helping to choose the picture for the cover.

Elisa Waldman – Thanks for helping me fix the first draft of my manuscript. I appreciate your friendship.

Maria, Donna, and Janice of KP Writer's Group – Your critiques helped make this a better manuscript. Thanks a bunch.

Friday night Girl Group (Jenny, Sheri, Sharion, Andrea, and Klarisa) – For your encouragement and valuable critique of chapter 1.

Joyce, my best buddy – For the water scene idea.

Farrah, my first editor – For challenging me to stop holding back the good stuff.

Patti, my second editor – For stepping in to provide final proofreading for this story's release.

Oaklyn Baptist Church – For your prayers and encouragement.

Colbie Caillat – For inspiring tunes.

God – For the ability to write out the stories in my head.

Billiard Buddies

Chapter One

Gina slouched on a bar stool and peered into the mirror behind the bartender. Her curls still held despite the perspiration streaming down her face. She tapped the counter for service. The bartender pushed a bottle of beer toward her while peeking over her head. Only one corner of his mouth curved upward in a sly smile. Glancing again toward the mirror, Gina studied a guy with a freckled face and business-cut red hair strolling up behind her. He seemed nervous, approaching with tentative steps while constantly looking over his shoulder. She'd just beat four of his friends, but Pete had never given up too easily. She'd known him for a few months now, and he'd always worked on his game or brought a new guy to test her skills. She wondered what his next challenge would be and hoped he'd raise the stakes.

Gina placed the bottle to her lips and welcomed the cool tingling sensation of frothy bubbles rushing down her gullet.

"Hey," Pete began. "How about some action on the next game?"

"Against whom?"

"Me."

"You sure?"

"Yeah."

Gina stared at the half-empty bottle in her hand before spinning on the stool to face Pete.

"How much?"

"One hundred," he answered, holding up a bill between two fingers.

After chugging the rest of her beer, Gina pushed the empty bottle toward the bartender and nodded to the billiard area. "Rack up. I'll start. You better have brought your 'A' game tonight because I'm not in the mood to lose."

Gina led the way and grabbed her cue which leaned against the far maroon colored wall. Her cue's multicolored rhinestone settings made it a sure deal that the men she challenged would never walk away with her prized possession. After Pete racked up the balls and positioned the cue, Gina inhaled, leaning over the table with acute concentration to prepare for her first shot.

"Hey, Pete. Maybe you should've begged to break. She always sinks at least two with her first shot," one of Pete's friends said from her right.

She smirked then, upon laying eyes on the cue ball, quickly refocused. She'd had enough of giving men chances. If she'd paid more attention to the signs from her ex-boyfriend, she wouldn't have had to walk in on him fooling around with some wench.

Her fingers tightened around the wider end of her cue while she slowly glided the other end between her index and middle fingers. Gina took a quick breath then pushed the cue forcefully toward the pale cue ball in her sight.

Bam!

Balls rolled in all directions, but only as she intended—one solid sunk in left center with another teetering on the edge of the far right corner pocket. Pete gasped. She frowned.

One extra shot then.

She headed to the opposite end. Her next shot required something special. She pressed her buttocks against the table and repositioned the cue behind her lower back. Sweat doused the blouse now clinging to her cleavage. The lights were especially scorching tonight. Gina's clothes clung to all the wrong places, and she realized the men were watching her rear end, rather than the game. *That's why they lose. They gawk at what they can* never *have.* She ignored their lustful gazes.

She glided the stick gently over her free hand, thrusting it toward the object of her fury when another glimpse of Hank with his woman flashed vividly through her mind. The cue tapped the teetering ball. Another one sunk. It was amazing how placing Hank's face on the ball helped her plant the shot.

Gina pushed away from the table and turned to face Pete. "You still sure about the action? You seem to be a nice guy. I'm giving you a chance to keep your money."

"I'm sure," he replied over the voices of his pleading friends.

"All right. Prepare for eight and out."

Without hesitation, she greeted each ball with the same intensity she possessed ever since she walked out on Hank a few months ago. She'd always been a decent player, but her broken heart made her unstoppable.

She sunk one right after another. Banked the fifth. Swerved the sixth. When Gina came face to face with the eight ball, she glanced toward Pete. His skin flushed a brighter hue than his exceptionally red hair. He'd been a good competitor, but not good enough. He'd brought many guys to beat her, but she'd bested all of them. Pete probably thought she'd be tired after playing three games against his friends and pounding down two beers, but she was only getting started.

Gina smiled and pushed her cue like it was a stiff feather. The eight ball sank without a hitch. She strolled over to the winner's basket to grab the hundred dollar bill. She earned it and a day at the spa is just what she needed. "Thanks for the game," she said. "Don't sweat it too much."

He never had a chance.

Chapter Two

"I think I've found your match. She's really great at pool, and she doesn't brag about it either," Pete said as he walked Sean from the parked cars to the bar which professionals in the area frequented.

"We'll just have to see if she's as good as you say," Sean said.

Pete beamed. He couldn't wait for tonight's game. Sean had proven himself to be a great player. Many times over, Pete would meet Sean elsewhere for a few games of pool, each time Pete coming up the loser. "If she beats you, you owe me a beer."

"Doubtful, but you've piqued my interest." Sean swung a bag containing his cue over his shoulder.

"I think you'll like her though. She's a neat person. Cute too."

"I hope this is not a matchup. You know I've already got someone." Sean raised his eyebrows.

"Of course not." Pete shook his head. "In fact, she's not looking either. Believe me, the other guys you'll meet and I have already asked. C'mon, we're running late."

When Pete O'Reily wasn't stuck managing accounts at a major bank downtown, he'd interact with Sean from time to time. Pete had great instincts when it came to people. Right away, he wanted Sean to be his friend. Not only that, Pete wanted the rest of the gang to like him as well. He was positive Sean's friendly disposition would win over a very reserved Gina Winslow. Perhaps that could be enough to throw her off her winning streak.

"Heeeeeey," came the boisterous yell from all four guys surrounding the pool tables spotlighted by bright white light.

Pete waved at his pals and beckoned Sean to follow along until Pete looked to his left and noticed Gina sitting by herself on a bar stool, her form silhouetted by the dim backlight.

"Be right there," Pete said to his friends. "I want Sean to meet Gina first." Walking over to the resident pool shark, Pete introduced Sean to her. "I'll give you a few minutes to get acquainted then the game is on." Leaving Sean and Gina at the bar, Pete joined the guys.

****

"I hear you play a mean pool game," Sean started. He couldn't help but agree that she was cute, her round 1920's features hugged by blond curls that bounced just above her jaw line when she turned to face him. Her smile accentuated her sparkling eyes.

"I heard the same about you. I think the guys brag too much. I love the game and practice a lot.

Where do you play? I've never seen you before," Gina said in a soft, velvet tone. She seemed guarded while she looked him over.

"I frequent another bar across town. Coworkers from the brokerage company I work for often go there."

She wrinkled up her nose. "Oh, you're one of those."

"Why? You don't like the business?" Sean asked, taking a seat next to her.

"It's just that the stock market is so, well, unpredictable. I just don't understand what's so fun about doing work based on guesses."

Sean thought of many other questions, but decided to not start waves this early. "Hmm. What do you do when you're not playing pool?"

"I teach kindergarten at one of the private schools in the area. Otherwise, I keep to myself." Gina glanced past him. "I think they're becoming impatient. Ready to play?" She stood and stepped toward the pool tables on the other side of the room.

Sean followed. "You bet. Rack 'em up."

"Best out of three?"

"Sure. Lady's first."

"Uh, Sean, that may be a mistake," Pete warned.

Sean panned the room to find shaking heads all around. "It's cool guys. I'd like to see what she's got."

"Your funeral." Pete backed away from the table.

Sean ignored his pal and nodded for Gina to take her first shot. After she pocketed four balls, Sean suddenly realized the prowess with which she played. Each shot possessed her full attention. Her stance never wavered once her study of the current layout was complete. The cue slid through her fingers as if coated with butter.
She's good. Too good.

Gina prepared for her second to last shot when Sean locked her gaze. He studied her intently until she broke their connection. Her jaw muscles were tight with tension, and her furrowed eyebrows betrayed intense concentration. She was angry, pissed off even. He checked the table to discover that her next shot would be difficult, but doable if the cue clicked the seven ball at just the right angle.

I have to distract her.

Sean moved, causing Gina to glance up at him once more. He grabbed the opportunity to smile. She grimaced before looking away and shaking her head. Gina readied for the next shot, but then faltered. For all her shots, he'd not seen her do that.

It worked.

She straightened and continued studying the table. Shifting to her right, she turned around and pressed her buttocks against the table.

Wow! No wonder the guys lose every game.

Sean forced his eyes to look away from her alluring figure and repositioned himself so he stood facing her side. Gina placed her cue across her lower back and faltered again. Finally, she took the shot. The cue nipped the seven ball, only nudging it a few inches.

Yeah! Beautiful!

Sean determined not to mess up the only shot she'd probably let him have during the game. However, as he surveyed the table, he realized, to his dismay, that his shot would be more difficult to make than hers. He'd have to hit the cue into one of hers to get to his. He had no intention of pocketing a ball for Gina.

He leaned over the table and exhaled before banking the cue ball into two of his, pocketing one.

I'm still in the game.

Sweat dripped off his chin as he made one shot after another. Then the unexpected happened.

She winked at him.

She'd used the same tactic he used on her and it worked. His heart pumped a bit faster, just enough to distract him for a split second. He stared at the ball teetering near the pocket and sighed. He knew she would pocket his ball in order to make her next shot, but that wouldn't help him. She wasn't going to mess up twice.

Gina won the first game bringing on a loud cheer from the others Sean learned she had consistently beaten over the past few months. Sean strolled over to her and gave her hand a congratulatory shake.

"Great game," he said. *That won't happen again.*

Sean waited until Pete finished racking up the ball for the second game. He avoided eye contact with Gina. She had unsettled him, and he couldn't figure out why. Shot after shot, Sean pocketed at least two balls. He'd have to bank the eight ball three times around her balls to make the last shot.

Sean, feeling a little pressure but not losing his concentration, focused on the small end of his cue and thought through the angle at which he'd need to tap the cue ball. No one made a sound. Sean could make out the newscaster on the television across the room. He blinked once to tune that out. Then he took the shot. The cue ball clicked the eight ball. The eight ball rolled past three balls to bank once, two more balls to bank again. Only then did he peer up at Gina to study her expression as he won the game. At least, that's what he hoped.

He quickly glanced down at the eight ball which had cleared all but one ball near the pocket he attempted to reach. He held his breath and focused intensely on the rolling ball until it slipped down the intended pocket.

He'd won the second game and did so without giving Gina a chance to shoot. He stole a glance toward Gina to find her tapping the broad end of her stick once, hard onto the floor. Her shapely mouth formed a frown.

"How about a coin toss to see who starts the last game?" Pete suggested, holding up a silver coin.

"Let me see that." Gina held out her hand.

"You don't trust me?"

"I don't trust the coin. I know you have one of those same sided ones." She flipped the coin over between her fingers. "Fine. Flip in onto the table. I choose heads."

With a smirk, Pete flicked the coin into the air. When it landed, Sean smiled when he noticed the bottom side up.

"My play. Pete would you do me the honor?"

"Sure, pal." Pete wasted no time in racking up the balls.
Every shot went flawlessly which worked to boost Sean's confidence that he might actually go home with bragging rights. The bar fell quiet while Sean

set up for the final shot of the third game for the win. He tapped the cue ball gently and watched it roll toward the eight ball. To his dismay, the cue ball nipped the eight ball at a bad angle sending itself into the pocket instead. Sean bowed his head in defeat. Boisterous celebration for Gina's conquest pervaded the bar with Pete most vociferous.

He walked over to her. "Great game, Gina. C'mon, I'll buy you a beer."

Gina smiled victoriously.

"I think you owe us all a round, Sean," Pete belted out in a slightly hoarse voice, red hair clinging to his sweaty face.

After paying for the drinks, Sean sat next to Gina to continue their conversation.

"I'm really impressed, Gina. I've never had to think that hard about a game. I'd like to play more often with you if you don't mind."

"I'd like that too, Sean. You're the first to beat me at a game during a match. I'm impressed with your skill. That last play could have happened to anyone. I consider it a fluke at best. I look forward to our next match."

When Gina finished her drink, she collected her things and said her good-byes.

"Are you leaving alone? Didn't you come with someone?" Sean asked.

"I didn't come with anyone here. They're all just friends. Besides, I don't live far. I'll be fine," Gina answered as she packed her cue away in a carrying case.

"I'd feel better if I walked you home. It's pretty dark out there."

"Suit yourself. I am *very* capable of taking care of me," she said, grabbing her cue's case.

"I don't doubt that, but I would hate giving you an excuse for missing our next matchup. Besides, I'd like to get to know my competition better." Sean smiled.

Gina smirked and nodded for Sean to join her.

"Pete, don't mess with my cue. I'll be back soon," Sean said.

"What? Don't you trust me?" Pete replied with a dash of Irish flare.

Sean merely laughed and followed Gina to the front door. She swung the case over a shoulder.

"May I?" he offered.

"Nope. No one touches my special stick but me."

"It's gorgeous. Did you have it custom made?"

"My dad carved it for me."

Sean placed a hand on the door latch, hoping she'd continue.

"Don't you have a girlfriend?" Gina asked. She changed the subject.

"Since when should that stop a guy from being a gentleman?" Sean asked as he pushed the door open.

"Point taken." She exited and kept walking.

Sean let the door slam shut so he could fall in step beside her. "So Pete told you about my girlfriend. What else did he tell you about me?"

"Enough."

Sean chuckled.

Gina glanced his way. "Nothing bad. He said you're a great guy."

"Hopefully, I can live up to that."

"Yeah. Hopefully." She turned her head forward.

She's tough all right. I wonder if she lets anyone get close. "How about you? Are you with someone?"

"No, and I kinda like it that way." Her tone soured.

Hmm. Bad move. "Okay. Next topic. Why did you wink at me during the game?"

She smirked. "Why did you smile?"

Sean shook his head and smiled. "Touché. You're good."

"So are you. I finally have a viable opponent. Will you come back?"

Cool. I've misread her. She's just cautious. "Of course. Who else am I going to sharpen my skills with?"

"You have a point. The other guys aren't that great. And, you're not a sore loser," Gina said as she turned at a corner.

"It's not often I get beaten, but to be defeated by a beautiful opponent isn't so bad. You played a great game back there."

"Thanks," she said and smiled, this time genuinely.

"How'd you get started?"

"My dad taught me," she answered and seemed to stiffen.

Now what? "Gina, are you always this serious?"

"No. I used to be more fun." She stopped walking and turned to face him. "Why does it matter anyway?"

Sean grinned at Gina. "You have no idea how thrilled I am to meet you."

"Thrilled," she repeated matter-of-factly. She furrowed her brows for an instant.

"I haven't lost a game in months. I just want to get to know the one person I can truly compete with."

Gina nodded and restarted their stroll toward her place. After a few more blocks, she stopped at the front door of a brick building.

"We're here. This is where we part ways."

"See you soon," Sean said and offered his hand for a shake.

Gina grasped his hand and shook once. "You bet. Thanks for the walk home."

Her touch affected him. After seeing her inside, he said 'good night' and returned to the bar to pick up his cue before heading to his car parked nearby.

Chapter Three

Over the next few weeks, Sean joined his new friends at the bar to play pool. As expected, Gina was his only viable rival in the game. He enjoyed talking to her during the down times as they waited for a free table.

Sean gulped a mouthful of beer before asking, "So what kinds of movies do you like?"

"Romance, except I think I need to change that. Real life doesn't seem to follow that formula." She sighed. "What's yours?"

"Adventure. I'm not into romance flicks, but I don't mind if it's worked into the film. Usually the timing's all off." He smiled.

"What about music? What's your favorite?" Gina asked.

"Rock, definitely. I love Rush."

"Rush? Never heard of them," she admitted.

"Really? Oh, man, if they ever come here, you have to go hear them. And you? What do you like to listen to?"

"I'm an easy listening kind of gal, but I usually get hooked if I can identify with the lyrics." She managed a dainty smile, and he glanced away to take another sip. Her response surprised him.

Gina's demeanor had been anything but easy whenever she held a cue between her fingers.

They talked about pool strategy, work happenings, other interests, and the interesting quirks they learned about the other guys while watching them play. Sean even mentioned his fascination with Game Boy although he had yet to own one. When they finally had the opportunity to compete, Sean found Gina a more relaxed, quite fun competitor. The cold shoulder she had given him the first time they played was nonexistent. They each won a game and decided to stop at a draw just for the night. Sean wanted to observe the others play for a while, and Gina agreed to sit with him at a table nearby. Her skin exhibited a radiant glow, and she giggled at all his silly comments about the mistakes Pete had been making whenever his turn to shoot arrived.

It was only when Sean brought up relationships that Gina seemed uncomfortable, becoming stiff as she twirled a lock of her already curly hair. He even mentioned that Cindy, his girlfriend, produced ads which sometimes made it to mainstream television or on billboards in the area. After observing Gina's warmth become frigid as displayed by her brusque responses, he refocused the conversation.

"I never hear you talk about a boyfriend," Sean said, hinting at his desire for more information.

"Because there isn't one," Gina said, hovering over her drink.

"I don't understand why not. You're an attractive woman and fun to be around," he noted.

"Sometimes, that's not enough. Sometimes, guys want more than I can offer," Gina admitted sourly.

"I bet I can find a guy who would like you just the way you are."

"Really. I don't need to be matched up. Friends of mine have tried before, but it never works out."

"Gimme a shot. I think I can pull this off."

Gina shot Sean a suspicious look, but quickly nodded. "You get one shot, okay?"

"Deal," Sean replied, offering his hand for a shake. She accepted his hand for a firm shake, but quickly withdrew. *I offended her. How can I get her to relax again?* "By the way," he began, "Pete is having a movie night at his place tomorrow night. Will you be there?"

"No, I try not to hang out at those. The guys all bring dates and I don't want to be a singleton hanging out watching everyone else cuddle. It's too much to watch," she said with a quirky smile.

"I understand. Cindy won't be able to go, but I already promised Pete I'd show up. It might be an early night for me."

"Speaking of an early night. I think I'll go home now."

Sean glanced at his watch to find midnight quickly approaching. Considering the guys often hung out until the bar closed at 2am, midnight could be considered 'early'. He smiled to himself.

"May I join you for the walk back to your building?" Sean asked, not wanting to seem intrusive. His father always stressed the importance of being a gentleman even when it's awkward. Although Sean knew Gina would be all right, he just couldn't bring himself to let her walk home alone this late at night.

"Sure. I enjoy our conversations. The company will keep my mind off my problems a bit longer."

Waving good-bye to their friends, Sean followed Gina out the door.

"Do you have family in the area, Gina?"

"No. I moved here after graduating two years ago. My parents died in a car accident while I was in college. I have no siblings. Sometimes, cousins will visit. Basically, when I'm not hanging with the guys, I'm visiting with my best friend Joanna uptown. How about you? Besides Cindy, do you have any family nearby?"

"No. I don't have anyone here either. I lost my father to cancer when I was ten, and my mom died from complications with pneumonia about a year ago. She had asthma."

"I'm sorry," Gina said solemnly.

Billiard Buddies

"I am sorry for you as well. From the way you handle a stick, I can tell you spent a lot of time with your dad."

"Yeah, I miss him a lot."

They walked in silence until they arrived at the front door of the apartment building.

Sean knew he should say "good-night", but ending on a sad note just seemed too depressing. "Do you mind if I walk you to your door? I hate ending our night on the loss of our parents. Maybe we can come up with something else to talk about in the few feet we have left."

"Agreed. Come on, walk me to my door," Gina responded with a slight emphasis on 'door'.

"I have just the thing we can talk about."

As Gina led the way to the second floor, Sean resurrected their conversation about favorite movies. "What kinds of romantic flicks do you watch? Drama? Comedies?"

"I prefer romantic comedies, but I also like science fiction space movies."

"That's cool. I have a soft spot for cowboy movies. Dad and I would watch them all the time on a Sunday afternoon. I also love all kinds of science fiction, especially those about vampires and werewolves."

Gina smiled and leaned against her door as she talked about her favorite scenes. He was enthralled by her love for life and the kids she taught every day. He wondered what could have happened in Gina's life to cause her to develop such a tough exterior whenever one of the guys at the bar approached. *Maybe that's why they look at me funny. I'm the only one she hangs with between matches.* Sean glanced at his watch to find he'd talked to Gina for another fifteen minutes outside her door.

Sean exclaimed, "Gosh, I'm sorry. I didn't realize we were standing here this long. Your neighbors must be wondering what the guy-who-won't-shut-up is still doing here. I better go. Cindy's probably waiting up for me."

Gina giggled while she unlocked the door. "The sound-proofing is really good in this building, so I don't think we were annoying anyone. However, I would hate to have your girl angry at me for delaying you. Have fun tomorrow."

"Thanks. See ya," Sean replied as he ran down the steps.

When Sean got home, he did not find Cindy waiting up for him. Instead, he found a note by the phone saying she had to return to work to finish up a template for an upcoming deadline. Frustrated, Sean dialed Cindy's cell phone.

"I thought you would be here. When are you coming home?"

"I'm sorry, Sean. I thought you would be out later than this. I really have to get this done. I should only be another couple hours."

"I'll be asleep by then. I'm tired. Don't forget I'll be at Pete's tomorrow night," Sean said dryly.

"I won't. I *am* really sorry I can't go. I do want to meet your new friends. Perhaps, next time."

"Yeah, next time. I love you."

"Love you too," Cindy said before the phone clicked into silence.

Sean stared at his cell for a moment before placing it gently on the night table on his side of the bed. He'd thought moving in together would mean spending more time with Cindy, but work meant more to her than he realized. After brushing his teeth, he fell into bed and slipped quickly into deep sleep.

Waking up the following morning around eight, Sean realized Cindy had never made it home as she promised.

What dinosaur of an ad is she working on this time?

Disappointed, he dragged himself out of bed and went to take a shower. By the time he was finished, he found Cindy curled up, still dressed, on the bed fast asleep.

Chapter Four

Memories of the previous few hours ran through
Sean's mind while he dressed for Pete's little
party. After running the normal weekend errands,
Sean had figured he could have lunch with Cindy
before she headed back to work for a presentation
of a newly released commercial she created.
However, by the time he arrived home, Cindy had
left, explaining in a note that she needed to get an
early start to prepare for the 'big names' attending
the event.

Sean sighed. *We don't even connect anymore.* He
sighed again and left for Pete's. After parking his
car, he realized Pete lived in the same building he
had walked Gina to a few times before. From the
apartment number, Sean knew that Pete lived a
couple floors above Gina. Taking the steps
circling the atrium, Sean walked passed Gina's
door and wondered what she would be doing all
alone on a Saturday night. He ignored the urge to
knock just to say "hello" and tramped quickly up
the next two floors.

The movie, of course, was a romantic comedy, to
appease the ladies.

Too bad Gina didn't come tonight. She would've
loved this one.

Pete had a wide assortment of alcoholic drinks
available. Due to Sean's slightly foul mood,
enhanced further by the movie's theme, he gulped

one drink after another. He grunted when the five couples started getting cozy in each other's arms to make out after the movie ended. Feeling somewhat awkward, Sean stood up and said "good night" only to find the door spinning around in front of him. He placed a hand on the door's frame to steady himself.

"Sean, why don't you spend the night? You don't look like you're in any condition to drive," Pete offered.

"Yeah, you're right. I didn't think I had that much. I'll ask Cindy to pick me up. See you next week." Sean rushed out of the door before anyone could ask him any specifics or remember that his girlfriend would be unavailable. He just couldn't spend the night in a place where five couples were going at it.

"Okay..." Pete managed to say before his date probably locked her lips with his.

Inebriated, Sean walked sluggishly down the staircase and found himself standing outside of Gina's door. *Great, how's this going to look? 'Um, I'm drunk. Can I spend the night?' She'll probably take one look at me and send me away. Why should she trust me not to try something?* Before he finished his thoughts, Sean's fist was already knocking on the door. He was so dizzy, he hadn't initially noticed the doorbell.

****

Cassandra Ulrich

Gina walked to the door and peeked through the peephole. She paused, unsure, but then decided to unlock the latch. Opening the door, she asked, "What are you doing here, Sean? Is everything all right?"

"I had a bit too much to drink at Pete's, so driving home is out of the question and Cindy's still working. He offered me a place to sleep, but I just can't manage being around the orgy happening up there. I hate asking you this, but could you spare a corner for me to crash? I'll leave first thing in the morning," Sean said, leaning on the doorpost.

"If you are as drunk as you look, you won't be up first thing in the morning. Come in, Sean. You can sleep on the couch." Gina wasn't sure she had made the right decision letting Sean into her apartment, especially in his current condition. Part of her felt like calling a taxi. Could she trust him to stay out of her room? However, when she stared at his face, Gina saw the sadness that probably prompted the drinking, and she felt sorry for her friend. She would just have to lock her door tonight.

"I really appreciate this, Gina," Sean drawled as she showed him to the sofa.

"Yeah, you owe me one. I'll get you sheets and a pillow. Don't throw up on my carpet, okay?"

Sean smiled. "I don't think I'm *that* drunk."

"I'll get a bucket just in case."

After Gina had brought everything and spread the sheets over the navy blue sofa, Sean removed his shoes and lay down.

"Did you call your girlfriend?"

"What?"

"Does Cindy know you're spending the night here? She might be worried."

"Oh, yeah. No, she doesn't know." He fumbled for his phone, but had trouble dialing.

"Let me help," Gina offered. Locating the number, Gina dialed and handed the phone back to Sean.

"Thanks."

Sean explained his situation and current location to his girlfriend. From the pained look on his face, Gina guessed the girlfriend didn't take it too well even before he dropped the phone onto the floor. Gina felt sympathy for Sean. He, either brave or stupid or trustworthy, had told his girlfriend the truth. Gina did not know any guy who would admit he slept over at a girl's apartment. Sean was one of a kind.

After turning off all the lights, Gina went to her room and locked her bedroom door. For extra measure, she blocked the door with a chair if he dared to pick her lock. Satisfied with her makeshift security, Gina slept soundly for the rest of the night.

The following morning, Gina woke up and walked over to Sean to stare at him sleeping soundly on her sofa. Sean didn't stir. He continued in his slumber even after she went to the kitchen to start coffee and fix breakfast.

****

Gina had asked, "Does Cindy know you're spending the night here? She might be worried."

At least that's what Sean thought she said. Foggy awareness brightened slightly in his mind. He couldn't believe Gina cared more about Cindy knowing his whereabouts than he did. Why didn't he care at that moment?

"Oh, yeah. No, she doesn't know," he said. His voice sounded weird.

His sight glazed over as he searched for his phone. All the numbers seemed to blur, so he tried feeling around for the button numbered two.

Man, I can't even see straight enough to speed dial Cindy. What Gina must think of me! It's been a while since I've done anything like this.

"Let me help," Gina offered.

"Thanks," he said, taking the phone back after she dialed his girlfriend.

Billiard Buddies

Cindy's phone rang five times before she answered.

"Sean, I'm in the middle of something. Is it important?"

"Sort of. I won't be home tonight. I had too much to drink," Sean said, slurring his words.

"Oh my goodness. Why would you do something so stupid? So, you're at the guy's apartment? What's his name? Pete?" Cindy asked, sounding annoyed.

"No, too many guests. I'm at Gina's."

Cindy gasped. "Is that the girl you play pool with?"

"Yeah, she's cool with me sleeping on her couch." Sean knew Cindy would be jealous. Perhaps, this unfortunate circumstance might heal their relationship.

"All right. I have to go." Cindy hung up.

Then again, it could have the opposite effect. Sean gently dropped the phone on the floor.

"She's pissed."

"I'm sorry. If you get up first, you can help yourself to anything in the kitchen."

"Thanks," Sean said as he drifted off to sleep.

Sean did not vomit, nor did he stir during the night. He did, however, wake up with a splitting headache. He stared past the kitchen at the off-white walls accented by renaissance paintings. It took him a moment to recall where he had slept the night before.

Sean's first thought was how he felt when Cindy hung up the phone. It hurt in his gut. Why was she so cold to him? He had explained his friendship with Gina over and over. How many times had he assured Cindy that he had no other interests?

As Sean became more aware of the coffee, eggs, and bacon aromas swirling in the apartment, he concentrated on pulling himself together and got up.

"Ow," he whispered holding his head. Glancing to the right, he spotted Gina in the modern kitchen with brown cabinets to the left of the front door. She flipped what looked like an egg before placing the pan onto the stove. Paintings of country scenes hung over a table next to the door on its right. The pastel colors had a calming effect on his pounding head.

"Good morning. If you can make it to the bathroom, I have aspirin in the medicine cabinet. However, if you like coffee, the caffeine should help the headache once it makes it through your system," Gina said from across the room.

Billiard Buddies

Sean dragged his feet across the living room toward the kitchen. "I'd like some coffee, but I do need to use the bathroom."

"Turn around, walk to the end of the hall, and go right. I left a new toothbrush for you next to the toothpaste. I keep some on hand for sleepovers, though usually it's for a girlfriend." Gina spoke to him slowly, yet firmly, as if to one of her kindergartners.

I guess I deserve that. "Thanks. I really appreciate this."

Sean stumbled once on the way and winced. *What a stupid thing to do!* He took a good look at himself in the mirror after brushing his teeth and washing his face. His usually well-groomed chestnut hair was a mess, and dark circles under his eyes made his tanned complexion appear sickly pale. He glanced around for a towel when he noticed a vase with fake daisies in an open ended wooden-house over the toilet.

"Where are the towels?" he yelled.

"Towels are behind you!"

Hearing Gina on the other side of the door, Sean grabbed a towel and dried his face. He sighed and mumbled, "You're a mess, Sean. How did you end up here?"

By the time Sean returned to the kitchen, Gina had already served breakfast.

"Have a seat. You'll feel better once you've eaten something."

"Gina, I never meant to put you on the spot like this. We've only known each other for a few weeks. I really appreciate your leap of faith in letting me crash here."

"And crash you did—right after you called Cindy. She was upset that you stayed here, wasn't she?"

"Yeah, she probably would have preferred if I stayed at Pete's, orgy or not."

Sean took a bite. He didn't want to talk about Cindy anymore, especially not with Gina. Things never bode well talking about girlfriend troubles with a female pal—too risky. *As if my staying here isn't risky enough.* "Mmm. The eggs are really good. What's in them?"

"Secret family recipe."

Sean giggled and then grimaced, once again holding his head.

"I guess that means only family can be made privy of the recipe," he said, trying to ignore the pain.

"That's right." Gina smiled and finished her breakfast. "Can I trust you to behave while I take a shower?"

"Yes, I'll work on finishing my breakfast."

Sean ate slowly, hoping the delicious food would not make an exit. He was finished by the time he heard Gina shuffling from the bathroom to her bedroom. Pushing up into a standing position, Sean placed each foot tentatively in front of the other until he had reached the sink with dirty dishes in hand. He struggled through his discomfort to wash all the dishes. Afterwards, he left the kitchen to put on his shoes and walk around a bit.

He'd been looking at some of the photos on display in the living room when Gina emerged from her bedroom, having replaced pajamas with outdoor clothes.

"Are they your parents?" Sean asked, holding up a framed photograph of an elderly couple.

"Yes. They were celebrating their twenty-fifth anniversary the day that photo was taken. They were gone a few weeks later." Gina turned toward the kitchen. She stopped abruptly, tilting her head as if confused while she looked the kitchen over. She returned her gaze to him. "You didn't have to clear everything."

"I know. Consider it a thank-you for letting me stay last night and feeding me a great breakfast. Again, I apologize for the state I came here in last night. I don't usually get sloshed. I'm a better judge of when to stop."

"You looked like you had a lot on your mind. I'm here if you ever want to talk. Here's my number if you ever need to call me."

Sean studied the number. "Thanks. I'll remember that. I'll give you mine too." He pulled out a card and gave it to Gina. "It's my business card, but my cells on there too."

"Thanks. See you next weekend?"

"Yes. Be ready to lose," he jabbed, grabbing his phone which still lay on the floor.

"Not on your life," she countered.

They both grinned and said "good bye". Sean closed the door behind him and walked slowly down the stairs.

When he arrived home, Cindy, apparently upset, stood waiting for him in the living room. Framed replicas of billboards she created acted as a backdrop. No matter where he turned, evidence of her craft pervaded their lives. Although Sean did not want to deal with it, he approached Cindy slowly and waited for her to begin.

"I can't believe you slept over at some chick's apartment!"

"Nothing happened," Sean responded in as calm a voice as he could manage.

"You expect me to believe that?"

"Well, believe this, Cindy. Gina and I had no more interaction than you and I have had in the past few months."

At first, Cindy seemed stunned, but soon began to cry. Sean waved his hand at her in disgust and went to the bathroom to shower. After he finished and left the bathroom, Cindy stood in the bedroom's doorway looking at him forlorn.

"Cindy, I'm sorry about what I said. It's just that it hurts you don't believe me. I wouldn't bother calling you or telling you who I was with if I was cheating on you. She's a good friend. That's all."

"You know I'm not well enough to be with you."

"Yeah, I know." *That's what you tell me. I wonder if you'll ever be well enough.*

Sean's thoughts flickered to the day Cindy first told him she had cancer. She'd originally thought she was pregnant and did not try to hide her disappointment. However, after a few tests, the doctor discovered a clump of cancerous cells in her uterus instead of a tiny harmless fetus that would grow into his child.

He shook his head slightly to rid himself of those painful memories and the feelings that plagued him because she would not let him touch her, not since…

He shook his head again, and said, "You're dressed. Are you going to work again today?"

"Yes."

Sean sighed. "Can you at least get back so we can go out to dinner together?"

"I'll try," she said, coldly.

Cindy kissed Sean on the cheek, got her keys, and left.

Chapter Five

Gina and the other guys were already in the bar an hour before Sean showed up. She sat by herself and bought a beer. When Sean finally arrived and headed toward her, she smiled.

"Hey, Gina. How's it going?"

"Pretty good," she replied. "The summer's going too quickly though. I'm not quite ready to go back to school yet."

She gestured for Sean to sit on the stool next to her, but he seemed somewhat agitated.

"Um, I was wondering, do the guys know I stayed over last weekend?"

"No, I didn't tell them." *And I have no intention of doing so. We'd never hear the end of it.*

"Good, I'd like to keep it that way."

Whew! At least we're on the same page. "Agreed. Things could get out of hand if they knew."

Gina called over the bartender and purchased a beer for Sean. Although he seemed to relax a bit after his first sip, something didn't seem quite right. She never wanted to get in the middle of anyone's relationship. However, it was too late to back out now. She helped a friend out. She'd have to deal with the consequences.

"How were things with Cindy?"

"Not so good," he said abruptly and took another sip.

She guessed he wasn't ready to confide in her and she couldn't blame him. She remembered all too well what it was like being the girlfriend, not knowing where your man's loyalties lay.

"Ready to get beaten?" Sean asked with a smirk.

"Ha ha," Gina laughed, deciding to let the tough subject fall away...for now. "You'll have a fight on your hands."

"Let's go then," he said, standing with an arm stretched out toward her.

Gina hesitated for a moment, but then took hold of his hand, allowing him to pull her onto her feet. She followed him over to the pool tables and grabbed the custom-made cue her dad made with multicolored gems circling the butt. Gina earned the first shot with a coin flip, and gazed briefly at Sean before setting up to take her first shot.

The game grew into a fierce competition. All the guys cheered Gina on as she made her shots, but booed whenever Sean made his. She found she had to choose her shots strategically. Even with her almost flawless plays, Sean often took advantage of any slight miscalculation. To her and everyone else's surprise, Sean won the first two games played leaving him the winner of the match. Gina stared at the table in disbelief. Had she become distracted by Sean and lost her edge? She racked her brain replaying each move to find the point where she lost the match.

"Now we're even, Gina."

Disappointed, Gina almost walked away without acknowledging Sean's victory. She didn't mind losing single games. But a match! That's never happened before, at least not in this dank little bar. She so wanted to fight the win. Instead, she extended her hand and said, "Well, played, Sean. You are a worthy opponent." She knew he earned it.

Shaking Gina's hand, Sean replied, "I know which shot messed you up, and it was a fluke. You would have had me if you got it."

Is he for real? No guy as competitive as he is would be so cordial. Where did he come from? "Thanks for trying to make me feel better, Sean. Let's try this again tomorrow, okay?"

"You're on."

Gina bought a round of beer for everyone before leaving. As usual, Sean walked her to the front door of her building before heading back to his car. She observed his car through a window in her apartment until he turned around a corner.

Why have you come into my life? You're the kind of guy I've always dreamed of, but I can't…I won't take you away from Cindy. It figures this would be my life.

****

Early Saturday morning, Gina received a call from her ex-boyfriend, Hank Crawford. She stared at the caller id and wondered if she should bother answering. All the pain she thought had passed resurfaced as she clutched her chest in agony.

Gina slowly extended her arm and grabbed the receiver. "Hello, Hank, what do you want?" she asked sourly. She'd hoped he would just leave her alone, especially since he was the one who cheated on her.

"Hey, Gina, I…I'm really sorry for what I did. It was stupid and inconsiderate. I was hoping we could start over."

"Start over? I gave you my heart and you stepped on it and turned away. I thought we were happy. Why did you have to break my heart? My heart can't afford another chance. We're done here."

"Wait! Don't hang up. I know your birthday is coming up soon and I wanted to give you something...something you always wanted from me, but I was too dumb to see how much."

"And you want to give it to me *now*? There's no way you get the chance. I don't even want to see you," Gina said in disgust.

Billiard Buddies

"Is there someone else?"

"That's none of your business. Leave me alone, Hank." She hung up on him. *I am so afraid to start over because of you. I've become a miserable human being.*

Hank kept calling for the rest of the day, but Gina ignored all the calls. Eventually, Hank's persistence got to Gina, so she picked up her purse and keys and left the apartment.

She went to the mall, hoping to pass the time before meeting Sean at the bar for their next match. However, the memory of her time with Hank and the way he cheated on her affections weighed heavily. Every few minutes, she found her eyes welling up with tears. By the time Gina headed for the bar, her cheeks were damp. She patted her cheeks dry but the moist sensation remained.

Being the first to arrive at the bar, Gina had no one she dared talk to for a distraction. Instead, she ordered a few stiff drinks and gulped them down. When Pete and a few others arrived, Gina was in no mood for conversation. She figured the guys would wonder if there would even be a match after seeing her current condition.

****

When Sean arrived, he found the guys huddled in a corner talking amongst themselves. Pete glanced up, shook his head, and motioned with a

41

nod toward a location left of Sean. Following Pete's nod, Sean noticed Gina hunched over an almost empty shot glass with six others stacked in a pyramid near her. He mouthed, "What's wrong with her?" to his buddy Pete who merely shook his head again as if in warning for Sean not to interfere. Sean could tell something was terribly wrong, and he wasn't about to let his new friend struggle alone.

"Gina?" Sean said, touching her shoulder. "What's the matter?"

"I don't want to talk about it." She sobbed. "I'm sorry, but I can't play tonight. I'm going home." Gina got up wobbly, nearly crashing into him. She began rummaging around in her purse.

"Gina, you know you can talk to me. I've never seen you like this," Sean said, filled with concern as he spread his arms out to catch her in case she fell.

"I've never seen me like this. Where are my keys?" She pulled something attached to a tiny cue ball, but it immediately slipped out of her fingers. "Shoot. I dropped them."

Sean made a motion to pick them up, but Gina pushed him away.

"No, I got it. I'm okay." Gina picked up her keys and stumbled toward the door, leaving her cue behind.

She's got to be out of her mind to forget about this.

Sean swung the case containing Gina's cue over his shoulder and said, "There's no way I'm letting you walk home alone like this."

"You never let me walk home 'lone. Why should be different t'nite?" Gina slurred.

Sean grabbed her arm and turned to the guys. "I'll be back after I drop her off."

Gina cried on and off during the walk to her apartment building. Sean had the time of it trying to get her up the stairs because she kept missing steps. So when they finally arrived at her apartment, Sean took the keys and opened the door himself. He walked her to the sofa and sat her down gently before leaning the cue case against a square wooden side table.

Sean knelt in front of her. "Gina, please tell me what's got you so worked up. What you've done tonight…I'm concerned."

"I don't know, Sean."

"Trust me, Gina. Whatever you tell me stays with me, okay?" he assured her.

She nodded. "My ex called today. All day. He wants to come back, but…" she trailed off.

"He broke your heart," Sean finished.

Gina nodded tearfully and exhaled heavily.

Sean sat on the sofa next to Gina and held her close, cradling her head. "I'm so sorry, Gina. I'll find someone for you…someone who cares about you."

Sean caressed the back of her head and tried to hush her crying, but Gina pushed herself away from his embrace.

"You should leave now."

Not understanding how he offended her, Sean asked, "Are you going to be okay? I mean, it looks like you've had too much to drink. Are you going to be sick?"

"Perhaps, but I'll manage."

"Call me if you do. It doesn't matter the time."

"Cindy wouldn't like that."

"You're my friend. Cindy'll just have to understand that. Promise you'll call me or I won't leave."

Sean figured he'd crossed a line when Gina glared at him, but then her gaze softened.

"All right. I promise," she said and immediately covered her face with both hands.

Billiard Buddies

Reluctantly, Sean got up and headed for the door. He glanced back at her once before walking into the hallway and closing the door.

Upon arriving at the bar, Sean assured the guys Gina would be okay. Instead of a matchup between himself and his sole competitor, they had to settle for being beaten by him in every game. He'd check on her tomorrow. Perhaps, she'd feel better about talking to him then.

****

Conflicting thoughts had flowed through Gina's mind when she allowed Sean to embrace her on the sofa. He was extremely loyal to his girlfriend, but also to his friends, even female ones apparently.

Then, he cradled her head and said, "I'm so sorry, Gina. I'll find someone for you…someone who cares about you."

I think you already have, Gina thought, *except I can't have him. He belongs to someone else.* She found herself falling for Sean as he caressed the back of her head. She had to push him away. She couldn't afford the pain that would come with not being able to have him. She never wanted to do what someone else did to her…break up a relationship.

"You should leave now."

Gina almost wished she hadn't said those words...almost.

After Sean left the apartment, she continued crying, but this time it was for the love she was discovering but could not pursue.
Time for my midnight bottle, she thought and played Colbie Caillat's song "Midnight Bottle" on her iPhone dock station to drown her sorrows.

The next morning, the phone rang, startling Gina awake. She found that she had passed out on the sofa after her final drink. *I'm starting such a horrible habit.* Gina cradled her head as she walked to the kitchen to look at the caller id. She noticed it was 9am. *Who can it be this early? Oh, it's...*

Picking up the phone, Gina said, "I'm okay. My head hurts, but otherwise, I'm fine."

Sean laughed on the other end. "I can only imagine the headache you are having this morning. It's *gotta* be worse than the one I had."

"Maybe," she said flatly.

"What are you doing today?"

"I figured I'd go to church."

"Church," Sean said the word somewhere between a question and a comment. "I didn't know you went."

"I haven't—not in long time, but after last night, it seems like a good idea. I need to be grounded. My ex's call shouldn't have unsettled me like that, but…"

"What? What did he say?" Sean said, concern apparent via his words. "My promise of secrecy still stands."

"I think he wants to propose. He said something about finally giving me what I've always wanted," she answered, deciding telling Sean the truth couldn't hurt anyone. At least, that's what she hoped.

"Do you want to? Marry him, I mean."

"No, but it hurt that he wants it a lot too late."

"So…where are you going to church? Cindy has to work, so I wouldn't mind joining you."

Relief flowed over Gina when Sean suddenly switched back to his original question. She bit her lower lip before giving him the address. "It's okay if we don't sit together."

"I know. I'll find you."

Gina hung up the phone wondering if she'd started something not so easily curtailed.

****

Sean found the gothic church building topped by two lion gargoyles without much difficulty. He also located Gina fairly quickly in the sparse crowd of elderly people, dotted with a few youths here and there. He sat in the same wooden pew, but not right next to her so as not to invite questions from the members. Sean nodded at Gina, and she smiled in return.

After the service, they met outside under a blue sky. It would prove to be a typical toasty August day.

"You look tons better than you did when I left you. I almost called to check on you last night," Sean said as they walked toward the sidewalk.

"Other than the headache, I feel much better. I can't believe I drank as much as I did. I can't believe I let him get to me that much." She sighed.

"Are you hungry? We could have lunch at the café across the street. We'll go Dutch," Sean offered.

"Probably not a good idea," Gina said, but her eyes said something different when she glanced at the café.

"You're right. I'll see you next weekend then." Sean started backing away tentatively. He understood why it was wiser not to be seen together, but he felt he could defend his position. After all, Gina was a good friend and he was just making sure she was all right. "Um, if you're hungry, we could do something else."

"I am *so* hungry, Sean. I didn't have breakfast, but…I really think I'd rather be alone right now. Rain check?"

Sean felt strangely drawn to her. He worried about her wellbeing, but didn't want to push her concerning this. "Yeah, maybe some friends could join us then."

"Yeah, that would be better. Thanks for everything. Bye."

"Bye," Sean replied and slowly turned toward his car.

****

By the time the following weekend rolled around, Sean could tell Gina was ready to take him on. The stakes were higher now. The guys decided that the champion title would go to the one who could remain victorious for two straight matches.

Sean knew Gina did not want to go out that easily. Her determination and concentration paid off. He was not able to win any games tonight. Gina had taken back her game.

They shook hands firmly. Sean smiled and hoped Gina could tell he wouldn't let her get the title easily.

When Sean arrived home that night, he was met by a disgruntled girlfriend.

"Where have you been?" she asked, sounding very upset.

"What do you mean 'where have you been'? You know where I am when I'm not home on a Friday night."

"Today was a hard day. I needed to talk to you."

"Then why didn't you call me? You know I would've come home if you called."

"I don't know."

"Tell me what happened."

"You know I told you that I have the chance to get the job in California if I do really well here. They liked the last ad I did for them, but were disappointed with the one I just produced. I'm really scared."

"I'm sorry, Cindy. I know how much this means to you. So, what happens now?"

"I have to work tomorrow night, so I won't be able to go with you to Pete's."

"C'mon, Cindy," Sean said, throwing both hands up in disgust, determined not to hide his disappointment. "Everyone's looking forward to meeting you. Why can't you take a break? You probably really need one."

"I know you're right, but I don't want to miss out on my dream because I didn't try hard enough. I will really make an effort to get to the next movie night."

Sean studied her for a moment, breathing deeply to calm himself.

"All right," he said. "I'm going to hold you to that."

"Okay. I'm headed for bed. Are you coming?"

"Yeah. Be there in a minute," he said solemnly and headed to the bathroom to brush his teeth.

Sean cuddled with Cindy as they fell asleep, but he couldn't help wondering if she was using her job to avoid hanging out with his friends.

****

Movie night progressed much the same as before except Pete showed a science fiction flick this time. That at least made Sean happier, but the hurt he felt about Cindy's continuing work schedule led him to drink too much, again.

As if living through a replay of the previous movie night, Sean headed down to Gina's and knocked on the door. Gina opened the door and invited him in without the initial interrogation.

"You know," Gina began, "we need to stop excessive drinking whenever we have relationship issues."

"Yeah," he agreed. He hated that Gina had to witness his lapse in good judgment yet again. He did not wish to take advantage of Gina's friendship or hospitality, although he felt totally comfortable around her. "Is it okay? I already left Cindy a message at home."

Gina eyed him suspiciously. She probably wondered why he didn't call Cindy's cell this time. "Sofa's available. At least you're not as smashed as you were last time."

"I'll try not to do this again. I don't like putting you on the spot like this."

"What are friends for, Sean? You were here for me when I needed one. It's okay."

"Thanks a bunch," he said, shoving his shoes under the coffee table. "I'm really glad we met."

"Me too."

Chapter Six

Pete found out about Gina's birthday and made preparations for a party at the bar. He and the guys decorated the pool tables with streamers and hung balloons from the ceiling. Pete knew Gina would already be in the throes of getting lesson plans completed, her normal schedule this late in August.

When Gina entered the bar, she seemed surprised at seeing decorations and Pete holding a bottle of Champagne. "What's this?"

"Happy Birthday!" all the guys yelled in unison.

Gina gasped. "How did you find out?"

"I have ways, my dear," Pete answered. He grinned because he had gone through a lot to find out. It's amazing what someone will tell the bartender when they'd had a bit of alcohol in them.

After they made a toast and ate some cake, Pete granted Sean the honor of presenting the gift to Gina, especially since Sean had picked out the gift. Sure, Pete had heard Sean and Gina both say they weren't interested in changing their current relationship status, but he also knew they would fit each other best if they just gave it a chance.

"We thought you could use this," Sean said, handing her a sealed purple envelope. Pete had also learned Gina liked purple.

She opened the birthday card to reveal a sizable gift card to a spa. Her laughter thrilled Pete. He could tell Sean was also pleased.

"They offer massages and other neat things. We hope you like it," Sean added.

"Guys, thanks so much. This means a lot. I guess this means no competition tonight."

"Next time. Tonight we dance," Sean said with a wide grin.

****

Pete was Gina's first dancing partner. Starting with him and ending with Sean, Gina laughed the whole time. However, when Sean took Gina into his arms, her heart fluttered just a bit. She had been somewhat tense, a bit on guard, with the others, but when Sean started dancing with her, she felt totally relaxed.

Sean gazed into her eyes, and said, "We wanted to make tonight really special. With school starting again, we figured we wouldn't see you as much." He seemed completely relaxed with her as well. The rate at which their friendship blossomed amazed her.

"You all accomplished your wish. I am very happy right now." Overcome by emotion, she buried her head in his chest. "I can't believe I'm crying."

Sean giggled. "Happy tears I hope."

"Yeah, they are," she said, gazing into Sean's soft brown eyes.

Suddenly, Gina's cell phone rang. Thinking it was a friend or one of her cousins calling, Gina stopped dancing to see who it was.

"It's Hank. Oh no! He got my cell number!"

"You okay, Gina? Maybe you shouldn't answer."

"If I don't, he'll keep calling." Gina answered the phone, but Sean stayed near. "Hi, Hank."

"Happy Birthday, Gina. I know you're wondering how I got your number. I called one of your cousins and declared I wanted to marry you."

She neared her breaking point. She needed to get rid of him and fast.

"Thanks for the birthday wish, Hank, but I have no intention of marrying you. It's over for us. Please stop calling me."

"I love you, Gina, please give me second chance."

Gina peered up at Sean, his eyebrows furrowed in concern.

"Gina, your cake is waiting," Sean interjected.

"I heard a guy's voice. Is someone with you?" Hank asked.

"Yes. I have to go."

"Is he your boyfriend?"

"Hank, I don't think you have the right to any information about my life. Please stop calling me." Gina hung up the phone.

"You okay, Gina?" Sean asked, again.

"I'm fine. Let's finish our cake. I'm sorry about the dance. I owe you one, okay?"

"You're on."

Gina ate her cake attempting to remain cheerful. However, she couldn't stop thinking about Hank's last question right before she hung up on him. She glanced quickly at Sean.

Why couldn't we have met when we weren't with anyone else?

****

Kindergarten was in full swing and still no one had earned the title of Pool Champion. Without fail, Gina and the guys met every weekend to compete, drink, and laugh.

Every time Sean walked Gina home, their friendship deepened to the point where she trusted Sean with her life. She even left a key for him outside her apartment door so he could sleep over whenever she was out of town for the weekend and he had too much to drink to drive home safely. He made use of the key twice during the fall months.

As the holidays approached, Pete invited Gina to plan Sean's birthday celebration in much the same manner as he had hers. The weekend before Thanksgiving, Sean strolled into the bar to a surprise "Happy Birthday" greeting.

After the toast and some cake, Gina walked up to him. "I believe I owe you two dances, Sean."

"I think you're right." Sean smiled and took Gina into his arms. Gina felt good being held by the guy who consistently calmed her worried heart.

They laughed and talked as they swayed to the slow songs. Gina's face flushed when Sean mentioned how beautiful she looked. "I think teaching agrees with you. During the summer you never looked as happy as you do when you finish a challenging week of dealing with five year olds."

"I really love my kids. They bring me a lot of joy. Someday, I hope to have kids of my own."

"You'll be a fun mom."

"What about you and Cindy? Do you want children?"

Sean smiled briefly. "I'd like kids, but Cindy's job may make that difficult. We'll have to adopt though. We're not sure she can...you know? Let's not get into that. You've worked hard to create a special day for me. Let's keep it that way."

"I'm sorry."

"No, you're fine. I'd rather not think about how complicated my life is...right now."

"Deal."

Gina could kick herself for bringing up Cindy. Sean never talked about his girlfriend, but Gina could tell things weren't so great. Nevertheless, he seemed to love Cindy enough to fight through whatever they had going on. Gina respected him for that. She wished her heart could manage the same allowances.

At the end of the evening, Sean walked her home and kissed her on the cheek, causing her heart to flutter again.

"Thanks for making this birthday memorable. I'm glad you're my friend. It's as if I've known you my whole life." Sean gently squeezed her hands.

"I feel the same way too."

****

Billiard Buddies

A few days later, on Sean's actual birthday, Cindy took him out for dinner and a movie. Up to this day, things had gotten very tense between them, and Cindy hoped to hold onto Sean by spending some time together on his birthday. Although Sean repeatedly assured her that his love for her was firm, Cindy had her doubts due to the growing friendship between Sean and his so-called billiard buddy Gina.

"Did you have a good time tonight?" Cindy asked.

"Yes, thanks, Cindy. I wish we had more nights like these. I miss spending time with you."

"I know, and hopefully all this crazy stuff will be over soon. I applied for the job in California and they are flying me out for an interview."

"That's great. When do you go?"

"That's the tough part. I leave the day after Christmas."

Sean frowned.

"Before you say anything, they actually wanted me to be there over Christmas. I told them I had an important engagement. I didn't want to miss spending time with you this holiday."

"How long will you stay?"

"I should be back by New Year's Eve." Cindy kissed Sean. "I need this. We need this."

"I need you more than any job. How do I know things will get better between us if you get this?"

"I'll make it better, Sean," Cindy promised and embraced him. However, she imagined Sean still had his doubts. She hadn't done such a great job keeping her promises lately.

****

Sitting alone in the living room while Cindy packed for her trip, Sean grabbed his new Game Boy and clicked the on button. He settled into the sofa intending to block his girlfriend's upcoming trip from his thoughts, but he clenched his jaw when he caught a glimpse of Cindy slipping into the bedroom, toothpaste and toothbrush in hand. Returning his gaze back to the electronic toy, Sean's thoughts rushed to his billiard buddy.

Christmas arrived quickly and Sean, heading for the bar, knew Gina looked forward to the temporary break she'd have from teaching. Although she enjoyed the invigorating energy the children endowed her, her mind and body needed time to relax. During the previous weekend, Sean, Gina and their pool buddies exchanged gifts via Secret Santa. The guys did not want to do this, but Gina insisted. Because she was the only female among them, they could not refuse her. Sean smiled at the thought of how much they catered to her though she'd never hesitated to beat them senseless at billiards.

All the guys had hoped they would get her name, but Sean was the lucky guy. He spent many days trying to pick out something that was practical, yet fun. Finally, he decided on a bracelet with two white gold ropes wrapped around each other. When Gina opened her gift, she loved it at once even before she knew who got it for her. But when she learned it was from Sean, she seemed extremely pleased.

"The two ropes of different design represent two friends. It's sort of like a friendship bracelet except that this is made of white gold, so it won't tear or tarnish. I hope you like it."

"I love it, Sean. Thanks."

Sean wondered what the other guys whispered while he placed the bracelet on Gina's wrist. He figured Pete would never let this one go, but it didn't matter. Gina had come to mean a lot to him, and he wanted her to feel special.

Other gifts were typical of guys: gift cards to Home Depot, movie theatres, tools, and the like. The only difference was Gina's gift for Pete which included a specialized cookbook and a wok. Sean smiled to himself. He could bet the wok would be used at the next get-together at Pete's.

When Sean walked Gina home, she surprised him.

"I have something for you. I didn't want the others to see, but I couldn't *not* get something for one of my best friends."

He accepted the gift from her and paused to gaze into her blue eyes when their fingers touched. She had come to mean a lot to him. He shook his head and refocused, ignoring the odd sensation in his gut.

"Thanks, Gina." He unwrapped the box to find a Game Boy. Sean laughed. "This is great. How did you guess?"

"Well, you talked about not ever having one. I figured I would give you a head start. I hope you like the starter cartridge I got you."

He stared at her intently. "It's perfect, Gina. You're the best. Merry Christmas."

"Merry Christmas."

Sean gathered Gina up into his arms. Her hands, braced against his chest, soon slid up and over shoulders to cradle his head and neck. She tiptoed with her chin snuggled inches away from his Adam's apple. He tightened his hold on Gina, drawing her close. Her warm breath tickled the hairs on his neck. He longed for this moment to last though he shouldn't. He eased away, forcing himself to gaze into her eyes. Smiling, he released his hold. Gina's eyes glistened moments before he nodded and turned, heading back the way they came.

The feel of her in his arms and the thoughts of her now warmed his skin. He blinked, tightening his grip on the Game Boy. He exhaled two shallow breaths.

Why did Cindy have to leave tomorrow? *I need so much to reconnect with you.*

****

"I don't know, Pete. I think I'll pass," Sean said.

"Oh, no you don't. I know Cindy'll be out of town for a few days. You could use the company, especially around the holidays."

Oh, why do you have to be right? Sean sighed. He didn't want to think about Cindy on her business trip. "Okay. I'll be there," Sean agreed. He often found it difficult to resist Pete's requests, but especially now that he felt particularly lonely.

Some other friends came over and played cards until rather late. Having learned from previous nights at Pete's, Sean only drank one beer all evening. He started cleaning up the kitchen when Pete brought in some empty dishes.

"Hey, Sean, thanks a lot. I really appreciate you cleaning up."

"No problem, man."

After placing everything on the counter, Pete stopped mid-turn and asked, "You know, I've been meaning to ask you something."

"Shoot."

"Is there something going on between you and Gina? The bracelet you got her was swanky. The guys and I were just wondering."

"Nothing's going on. She's a great friend. You were right when you said I'd like her. She's become one of my best buds."

Pete shrugged. "Okay, sounds cool. We were just wondering. Thanks again for cleaning up."

Sean watched Pete leave the kitchen and hoped his pal wouldn't start any rumors. He had enough trouble without Cindy hearing whatever the guys would dish up.

When card games came to an end, Sean said "good night" and headed down the stairs.

At first, he intended to go home, but the thought of being alone did not appeal to him. As Sean passed Gina's door, he paused and knocked before he thought through what he was doing.

Gina opened the door. "Sean, what a surprise!" She eyed him closely. "You don't seem drunk."

Now, I've done it. He couldn't even rationalize why he felt compelled to see her. Even with her prowess during billiard games, he'd always felt comfortable around her.

"I'm not. I…uh…I didn't want to be alone. Cindy went to California today on a business trip. Do you mind if I stay here tonight?" He suddenly became nervous he'd finally crossed that line.

"No, not at all." Gina opened the door wider so a relieved Sean could enter.

When Sean peeked into the apartment, he noticed someone sitting on the sofa. "Oh, I didn't know you had company. I'll just go home," Sean said as he stepped back.

Gina grabbed his hand and pulled him gently into the apartment. "Don't leave. It's okay. He's my cousin Gene visiting for the holidays."

"I don't know why I'm here. Are you sure it's okay?"

"Yes. Stay."

Sean took a closer look at Gina's cousin and his jaw dropped in surprise. With a neon-green jacket over a deep red dress dotted with colorful five-pointed stars, and multicolored striped stockings that frolicked with ruby slippers, her cousin reminded him of a rainbow.

"Hey sweetheart, don't be a stranger. I promise I won't bite." Gene smiled as he sauntered across the floor toward Sean. "Any friend of Gina's is a friend of mine." He offered his hand to Sean as if expecting a kiss.

Sean reached for Gene's hand and shook it instead. Sean released Gene's hand and smiled at Gina.

"My cousin is very…flamboyant, but he's harmless. He doesn't always dress like this. He does it for the shock value. Gene, you'll sleep on the floor in my room so Sean can have the sofa."

"Cous', you are *not* thinking about putting *this* body on the hard floor."

"Actually, Gene, no. I have a sleeping bag for you. I think you'll manage."

Sean pulled Gina aside while Gene ranted about the change of plans. "Are you sure about this?"

"Yes, Sean. Stay and sleep on the couch. No one should spend the holiday season alone. I'm glad you came."

****

Faint giggles from Gina's room woke Sean with a start on the sofa. Still groggy from the late night conversation with Gene, Sean opened his eyes and stared at the rays of light from the early morning sun dancing on the ceiling. He couldn't thank Gina enough for declaring an end to the evening, drawing Gene off to her room. He smiled thinking about the awkward greeting of the previous night. Gene was indeed a character, but one who could turn into a good friend provided he behaved himself. Soon, his thoughts turned to figuring out why he couldn't walk pass this apartment.

What am I doing here? I can't keep this up. She's a great friend, but I need to stop taking advantage of her kindness.

Just then, a door swooshed open at the far end of the apartment. Sean observed Gina, an alluring sway apparent under a robe, as she approached on slender bare feet. From the dark ring under her eyes, he guessed Gene did not let her sleep. Nevertheless, her cheeks glowed with a natural blush, her full slightly puckered lips, a luscious pink. Gina paused next to the sofa and smiled, boring into his soul with her gaze. His gut clenched. He swallowed hard. There was no denying the warmth he felt gazing up at her lovely face.

"You're up early. I see you changed your point of view."

"Yeah, your cousin makes me a bit nervous. I wanted to be able to see who was coming out of the bedroom."

"I know. He likes making straight guys nervous."

"You're wearing the bracelet," Sean said as he moved his hand to touch Gina's fingertips.

"I'll never take it off. I like it a lot." Gina's hand shivered at his touch, or was it his that trembled? "I'll start breakfast."

Sean's fingers slid away from Gina's as she walked away toward the kitchen. He brought his hand to his face and touched his lips thoughtfully. He felt warm inside. *I can't come back here.* Sean sat up for a moment before heading to the bathroom to wash up. After drying off, he joined Gina in the kitchen and leaned against the counter next to the stove where she was cooking.

"Gina, I won't do this anymore, staying over. I can't keep taking advantage of your hospitality." Sean pulled a key out of his pocket. "Here's your key. I forgot to give it back to you when you returned from your trip."

Gina stared at Sean, her head cocked to one side as if confused. "I don't mind you staying over when you need to. You don't have to stop."

"I need to do this."

"Because of Cindy?"

"Yes, and because of me." Sean placed the key on the counter and walked away.

****

Why do I feel like he just broke up with me? Gina looked over at Sean who had begun gathering his stuff. "Won't you stay for breakfast?"

Billiard Buddies

"I don't know..."

"Please stay for breakfast. It's almost ready. At least let us enjoy our last slumber party breakfast."

Sean paused and seemed to think it over for a second. "Okay, I'll stay. I owe you that much."

"Mmm, baby, what smells so good?" Gene asked as he entered the living room.

"My specialty, Gene baby, so sit down and enjoy," Gina replied.

"You don't have to tell me twice. C'mon, Sean, hurry up and sit before my eggs get cold."

Sean shook his head and smiled at Gina.

My gay cousin and my best friend who's suddenly afraid to sleep over—this is going to be an interesting meal.

As his custom, Sean complimented Gina on her breakfast and thanked her for letting him stay over yet again. Gene flashed Gina a questioning glance with a quirky smile, and she could swear her face turned red.

"Gina, I better get going," Sean said and stood to clear his dishes.

"Can I delay you just a bit to join Gene and me in a family tradition?" Gina asked.

"What is this tradition?"

"When my cousins and I were little, we would dance together on the second morning after Christmas," Gina explained.

"Where's the music?"

"It's in your soul, baby," Gene answered. He started moving his hips to unheard Spanish music.

"The CD player is on a timer. We start by dancing to the music in our heads, then when the music starts playing, we change our timing to match what's playing. Like this." Gina started to dance throwing her hands into the air as she jumped around.

"I don't know, Gina. This is weird. I feel like I'm in grade school." Sean laughed.

"Try it. It's really fun," Gina encouraged.

Sean started moving as if to a rock song, playing air guitar and drums. By the time the music started playing, they had been dancing for a few minutes. Slowly, their motions merged into the rhythm of the song. First, Gene grabbed Gina's hands and danced with her.

When Gene finally let her go, Sean grabbed Gina around her waist and started to slow dance. Their eyes locked as they danced until suddenly they weren't dancing anymore. They stood still gazing into each other's eyes.

Sean licked his lips and released Gina. "I need to go now. Thanks for this. It was fun," Sean said abruptly. He seemed uncomfortable and confused. "See you at the bar, okay?"

Gina knew something strange had happened. It felt great, but it's what she fought to avoid these many months. She watched Sean glance around until he located his keys and phone. He seemed nerve-wrecked.

"Okay. Have a Happy New Year."

"You too…both of you." Sean got his coat and headed for the door.

When he left the apartment, Gina locked the door and leaned against it as she slid to the floor, crying.

"Honey, why didn't you tell him how you feel about him?" Gene admonished.

"I can't, Gene. I *won't* be the other woman. I know what it feels like losing the man you love to someone else and I won't do that to Cindy."

"Gina, it's obvious he cares about you. He should know how you feel."

"No, Gene, and you're not allowed to say anything to him, you understand? He still loves Cindy."

71

"Girl, he's a great catch."

"He's my friend, and I won't give anyone reason to claim I snared him in some net. I'll suffer silently so he can have the love he desires."

"Are you sure he's so happy with her?"

"It doesn't matter. If he ever leaves her, it won't be because of me. He has to choose for himself without interference from me. I won't be party to his breakup with her, no matter how much it hurts."

****

On New Year's Eve, Gina met with her friend Joanna to hang out for the evening. "Wow, Gina. This is beautiful. Where did you get it?" Joanna asked as she reached out to touch the bracelet on Gina's wrist.

"Sean, my sparring pool buddy, gave it to me for Christmas. He was my Secret Santa."

"From the look of this bracelet, he seems to be more than that."

"No, Joanna, he has a girlfriend whom he loves very much."

"What about you? How do you feel about Sean?"

Gina sighed. "I love him, Joanna. It's so hard for me to stay out of the way."

"So…he's doesn't know how you feel."

"No, I never told him. But something happened to him when he stayed over with Gene and me. It seemed he felt attracted, but he's probably afraid it'll ruin our friendship. I'm such a mess. I can't believe I'm sad because he won't sleep over. It's not like we've been anything more than good friends."

Joanna pursed her lips. "Well, hopefully he figures it out soon. You deserve so much more than what you've been handed." Joanna picked up her glass. "Let's make a toast to Sean realizing who his true love is and that it's you."

Gina clinked her glass with Joanna's and sipped her drink thoughtfully.

I really hope you're right.

Chapter Seven

On Valentine's Day, Gina arrived home from school to find a yellow carnation and a card leaning against her door. She picked up the items and opened the card which read, *Gina, thank you for being a great friend. I feel good when I'm around you. I hope this day brings you happiness and love from an unexpected source. Your pool buddy, Sean.*

She wondered briefly how Sean got in, but then recalled that although he returned her apartment key, Sean had kept the key to the apartment building's main door.

While Gina thought over how much she missed Sean's unexpected sleepovers, a noise startled her. She looked up and lost her breath.

"Hi, Gina. Happy Valentine's Day."

"Hank," she said, almost breathless, "what are you doing here? How did you get in?"

"You have friendly neighbors." He smirked. "I wanted to give you your special gift," he said, reaching for a pocket inside his jacket.

"Hank, I don't want it. Please leave me alone."

Hank pulled his hand out his jacket and frowned. "Who gave you that flower?"

"A friend, Hank, just a friend." Gina could feel tears well up on her lids. This man who had successfully broken her down would not cease invading and destroying whatever happiness she latched onto.

Hank grabbed the flower and ripped it off the stem. Crushing it, he threw it down the center of the stairwell.

"No!" Gina screamed.

Hank grunted. "He must mean a lot to you. I asked you if you had a boyfriend. Why did you lie to me?"

"I didn't lie." She paused and backed into the door. "I didn't say."

"I still love you, Gina." He grabbed her arm and pulled her close to land a kiss, but Gina shrugged away, forcing Hank to release her. He huffed then whispered, "I'll be back," before stomping down the steps.

After Hank exited through the main door, Gina shook all over. She quickly unlocked her door and rushed inside. Her phone rang a few moments after she shut and relocked her door, causing her heart to pound harder against her ribs. It was Sean.

"Hello," she answered, her voice shaken.

"Gina, what happened?"

"Hank was here. He was angry. He crushed your flower."

"Are you okay? Did he hurt you?" He sounded anxious.

"I'm okay. He didn't hurt me. I'm scared. He got into the building. He knows where I live," she rattled.

"Do you need me to come over?"

"No. No, I'll be fine," she said, but she really wanted to say the opposite. She wished it would be all right if he came over, but she knew his visit would end in disaster for his Cindy. No, it was better he stayed away…especially now.

"I'm so sorry this happened to you. I hoped today would be a happy day for you."

"Me too." Gina took a deep breath. "I'm glad you called when you did. Thanks for the gift. It means a lot."

"I'll check on you tomorrow, okay? If you think you need a restraining order, by all means get one."

"Okay."

"You sure you'll be all right."

"Yes, Sean. I'll be fine. Go on and enjoy your night with Cindy. We can talk tomorrow."

"Please call me if he comes back."

"I will. Now go, and don't worry about me."

He sighed audibly. "Fine. Bye, Gina."

"Bye, Sean," Gina said and hung up the phone.

****

After calling Gina, Sean remained seated in his car debating whether he should keep his plans with Cindy or rush over to Gina's apartment. Merely considering these thoughts bothered him. He struggled over his options, and in the end decided he'd take Cindy out for Valentine's Day dinner as originally planned.

Sean picked up his girlfriend at six o'clock and drove over to the restaurant where they had their first date over a year ago. He helped her out of the car and placed his hand at the small of her back as they entered the dining area. Sean grabbed a bouquet of red roses waiting at their table and handed them to her.

She simply glowed. He smiled, pleased he'd decided to keep the dinner reservations.

"I love you, Cindy. I hate the fact that we've drifted apart. I want to feel close to you again."

"I love you too, Sean. I'm sorry I've been so unavailable. Things will get better."

She reached across the table to hold his hand. He smiled, but knowing she'd made these promises before left him disappointed.

"Cindy, when do you think we could invite Gina over? I would really like you to meet her."

"I don't know, Sean. Will she bring a date?"

"I don't know. Is that necessary?"

"For me, it is."

He clenched his jaw. Cindy continued creating a huge deal out of a casual hang out. *Why does Cindy want Gina to be connected to someone else so badly?* He twirled his empty fork between his fingers, and gradually released a pent up breath. Gina would probably balk at having to find someone to come with her, but maybe Pete could grant him a favor. Pete could be harmless when he had to be.

"Okay, I'll tell her. Let me know when you're available."

"Okay," Cindy replied as she took a sip of wine.

When Sean and Cindy arrived home, he grabbed her purse and threw it onto the coffee table. He wrapped his arms around her and tenderly kissed her mouth, neck and face. At first, she gave in to his passion, but eventually pushed him away. Sean reluctantly released her.

Billiard Buddies

"Cindy, do you think we can…"

"Um, not just yet," she said, interrupting his request.

"I'm trying to be patient. I know you needed time to heal, but…how much longer before I can touch you?"

"I just need a bit more time."

Sean backed away and gazed into her eyes.

"Do you not want me, Cindy?"

She kissed him again.

"I want you. I'm just not ready. I had a big scare with the cancer. I know you've been patient. Please, Sean, just a little more time."

Sean sulked away. He knew physically she was all right, but the battle had taken its toll on her emotions. So, although he had hoped that on a night like this, she would make an exception, apparently love making would not be forthcoming. He hardly slept as he held her close in his arms.

It probably would have been better for her if I hadn't moved in a few months after we'd met. Looks like it would've been better for me too. I can't keep this awkward living arrangement. Maybe she'd feel better if we got married.

****

The next day when Gina arrived home from work, she noticed Sean had left a replacement flower for her. She smiled as she smelled the aroma. Upon entering her apartment, she walked over to her answering machine and found she'd missed a phone call. She listened to her voice mail. She wasted no time in returning Sean's call as he requested. Her heart warmed when he said "hello".

"Hi, Sean. You didn't have to replace the flower, but thanks."

"I found the other flower he crushed. Are you sure you are okay? I mean, would he hurt you?"

Oh, how calmingly sweet his voice sounded.

"I don't think so."

"Why was he so angry with you?"

"He thought I lied to him about having a boyfriend. When he saw the flower, he went crazy." Her heart jumped when she said the word "boyfriend". She hoped Sean wouldn't get weird.

"Oh. Hmm." Sean paused. When he spoke again, warmth infused his words. "Sorry my gift caused you trouble."

As always, Sean remained grounded. She couldn't determine if he experienced a similar attraction to her that she felt for him.

"I wouldn't change anything. Your gift was great."

"Call me if he shows up again."

Gina heard muffled sounds. She wondered who Sean spoke to on the other end. She wondered if it were Cindy.

Gee, what if she's angry I called him?

"I better go. I'm still at work."

Oh, good, it's not her. "Okay. See you soon?"

"I can't meet at the bar for a couple weeks. I'm travelling to meet with clients, but I'll get in touch when I return. My being away doesn't exempt you from calling if he returns, okay?"

"All right. Bye, Sean."

"Bye 'til then. Stay safe."

His last two words lingered in her mind hours after they were said. She missed him so much it hurt.

****

A few weeks later, Sean set up a meeting to talk to a guy friend of his about going out with Gina. Sean wondered if he would be doing this if Gina even so much as hinted that she had feelings other than friendship for him. But he couldn't...shouldn't go there. He'd devoted himself to Cindy. She's the one he wanted to marry.

Cassandra Ulrich

However, he also cared deeply for Gina and hated seeing her alone and unhappy. *If I wasn't attached...* He smashed that thought away when Greg asked him why they'd gotten together.

"So, Greg, do you think you could meet her? She's really neat," Sean said.

"Yeah, sure. I'll go out with her. You said you've been to her apartment?"

"A few times. So, when should I tell her you'll take her out?"

"Friday. Here's my number. If she's interested, have her give me a call."

Sean called Gina that night to tell her about the date with Greg.

"I'm not so sure about this. I'm fine with my life. Too much trouble and drama, dating and stuff," Gina said.

"Oh, no you don't. You said you'd gimme one shot at getting you matched up."

She sighed.

"You're right. I did say that. All right, give me the guy's number."

"His name is Greg."

"Right. Greg. I'll call him tomorrow."

Hopefully, things will work out for you and Greg like they did for me when a friend introduced me to Cindy. Sean sighed as he ended the call.

****

Greg arrived to pick Gina up in time for an early dinner. She waited outside to avoid having to buzz him in before they left. Greg smirked when he got out the car and met her halfway up the walkway.

"Absolutely stunning! You must be Gina," he said, his hazel eyes sparkling in the evening sun. Nothing would disturb his sculptured slicked back hair style accented by the Armani suit. He had perfectly manicured nails and eyelashes any woman would pay too much to imitate. He must not play pool. No avid pool player could maintain such beautiful fingernails or see the cue ball clearly with those…those lashes.

"Yes," she admitted, returning a smirk of her own. She'd have to behave. Sean at least got a good looking guy for her. "And thank you. It's great meeting you, Greg. So where are we headed?"

"Do you mind if I keep that to myself a bit longer? I'm hoping to impress you."

Gina raised her brows. She'd make an attempt to be nice. "All right, let's go."

After twenty minutes of driving, Greg parked in a lot next to Morton's The Steakhouse. Yes, he impressed her. He offered his hand to help her out of the car.

"So, what do you think so far?"

She smiled. "So far? Very nice."

At first, things progressed well enough. Conversation was kept simple and light. Gina did her best not to bring Sean up, and Greg followed her lead.

When they were done with dinner, Greg took Gina to walk along the pier. The air was crisp and the sky, clear. He slipped his arm around her shoulder as they looked up at the stars. His slight caresses made her a bit uneasy, but she didn't push his hand away.

When Greg took Gina back to her apartment, he tried to coax her to invite him inside. However, she'd made a promise to herself long ago that no one would be invited in on the first date.

"Well, good night, Greg. Thank you so much for a great evening." She turned to unlock the door, but he didn't move away. "What are you doing?" she asked.

"Aren't you going to invite me in?" Greg pressed.

"No. You're likeable, but I'm not ready to let you into this part of my life." She gently pushed his hand off the doorpost.

"You let Sean in, but you won't let *me* in?" Greg pushed Gina against the door and tried to kiss her.

She pushed against his chest with all her might. "It's not *like* that between us. You need to leave. You can forget about another date. Get out!"

Greg smiled slyly and then willingly left the building.

Gina fumed. *How dare he! What did Sean tell him about coming over?* "Arrgh!" Gina slammed the door shut and locked the bolt.

****

The following night, Gina stepped into the bar to find Sean had not yet arrived. All the guys present avoided her after she gave them what she hoped was a cross glance. They must have guessed from Gina's demeanor that she was pissed off, all hoping it was not them by the way they whispered to each other. When Sean entered the building, she stiffened her posture to express he was in for it.

"Hey, Gina, how was your date? Greg left me a message explaining that the date went sour, but he didn't give any details. I wanted to talk to you first before returning his call."

She glared at him, and said in an angry whisper, "What did you tell him about us? He tried to force his way into my apartment claiming I should let him in like I let you in."

"I didn't tell him much, just that I saw your apartment. What do you mean he forced his way in?"

She started to tear up. *Don't cry, Gina. Please don't cry.* "I told you not to do this, but you insisted. Well, you had your chance. No more match ups, ever."

"Gina, please." Sean reached out to her.

"Don't touch me," she said, raising her voice, arms flung over her head. "I am *so* angry at you right now. I told you things *never* work out for me, but you…wouldn't…listen." She grabbed her purse and started for the door.

"Let me walk you home. I want to talk to you about this," Sean begged, following her to the door.

"No, you don't *get* to walk me home tonight. Leave me alone."

She looked passed Sean to glimpse the guys still watching the argument unfold as it continued outside.

Gina walked as quickly as she could toward her apartment. She heard Sean yelling for her to stop, but she would not relent. She could not face him now. She needed the space. She had no idea for how long, and that thought ached in her heart.

Betrayal overwhelmed Gina as she ran up the stairs to her apartment. When she entered her space, she could still hear Sean calling her outside the windows overlooking a small garden. He finally stopped after she refused to acknowledge him.

An hour later, Gina's machine began recording a message from Sean. Everything in her pushed her to answer the call, but she could not give in to her fragile emotions. After hearing his desperate words emitted from a solemn yet velvet voice, her resolve broke. Unfortunately, Gina reached for the phone just as Sean hung up. She brushed her fingers over her bracelet. *Oh, Sean, I love you so much.*

****

Sean called out after Gina as he followed her, but kept his distance. Gina didn't stop, nor did she turn to look at him. He soon found himself outside the main door of the apartment building, wounded and confused. He had hurt her by trying to interfere and so may have lost her and the close bond they shared as friends.

Sean ran around to the side of the building where Gina's windows overlooked a garden. "Gina, please talk to me." He saw her peer out a window. "I'm sorry," he said with strain in his voice.

Gina closed her window, but Sean paced for a few more minutes, running his fingers through his hair. The thought of losing her friendship pained him.

Gina. I never meant to hurt you. Why won't you talk to me? This hurts. Feeling dispirited, Sean headed back to the bar. He kept glancing back, hoping Gina changed her mind and would come running after him. *I don't want to lose her friendship.* Sean sighed deeply, continuously. He felt short of breath. His insides hurt everywhere, and tears started to form.

When he arrived at the bar, Sean explained to the guys he needed to go home.

"Is she okay?" Pete asked.

"No. Her date with Greg went badly. I'm going to call and slam him. I'll see you guys later."

Sean left in a hurry, his face on fire. He sped home, hoping—this once—Cindy wouldn't surprise him by being there. After Sean dashed into his apartment, he called Greg. Sean did not wait long enough for Greg to finish saying "hello".

"Why didn't you tell me you tried to bang her?"

"I was angry that she wouldn't put out, man."

"Why would you think she was that kind of girl?"

"Well, you said you went to her apartment a few times. I just figured…"

"You figured wrong, Greg! Why didn't you just ask me?"

"You didn't seem the kind of guy to kiss and tell."

"You're such a loser, Greg! You were out of line! I picked you because I thought you were a decent guy. I am *so* angry. You'd do well to avoid me for a while so I don't *bash* your face in."

"Are you sure you don't have the hots for her?"

"She's my friend. That's all. I care whether she's happy or not."

"Well, you defend her like she means more to you," Greg said.

Sean grimaced, unsure how to respond. Had his care for Gina exposed something more? First, Pete questions him about his relationship with Gina, and now Greg. Has Gina been wondering too?

"I'm sorry, Sean. I knew you really wanted this to work. See you around."

Sean hung up the phone and bit down on his lower lip. He swore he drew blood in doing so. He immediately covered his face with his hands and slumped onto the sofa. He hunched over, dropping his head onto folded arms and groaned. He didn't move until his back hurt.

When he finally pulled himself together, he called Gina. The house phone rang, but the machine picked up. "Gina. Please pick up. I know you're hearing this. Gina. Gina. I told him off. Please.

I'm…so…sorry. My friend. Arrgh. Pickup, pickup. I know you're there. C'mon. Okay. Bye." *I miss you.*

Gina never answered nor did she return his call. He wondered if he'd finally crossed a line he could never erase. Sean remained in a daze for the next three hours.

When Sean locked Cindy's gaze as she entered their apartment later that night, she took pause and brought her hand to her chest.

"I didn't expect you home so early. Didn't you play pool?"

"No. I'm not up for talking right now. I'm gonna just go to bed, okay?" he said, his tone somber.

"All right. Let me know if you need anything or just wanna talk."

He was grateful she remained quiet as she lay next to him in bed, leaving him to brood in peace.

****

Sunday morning, Sean got up and made a store run. He soon found himself at Gina's apartment. He still had the key to the building, so he let himself in. When he arrived at her apartment, he used the doorbell for the first time since he had been visiting her.

Gina opened the door slowly, and Sean extended his hand with a package.

"A peace offering."

She accepted it and opened the package to reveal a lavender candle. "Come in."

He followed her into the apartment and closed the door behind him. After Gina lit the candle, she walked toward Sean and stopped a few feet away. Her gaze held sadness which pulled at his heart. He closed the gap and gave her a bear hug. She also wrapped her arms around him.

"I'm sorry I yelled at you," she said after a couple minutes.

"Don't be sorry. I deserved it. I was cocky and so sure I could solve all your problems. I'm the one that should be sorry." Sean released Gina and held her hand as he led her to the sofa. "I didn't mean for you to be, ah…um…" He gazed into her eyes and continued, "…forced to do something you didn't want to do. He misunderstood our relationship. I did not mislead him on purpose. I need you to believe that."

"I do."

"Tell me something. What's the *real* reason you don't want to go out?"

Gina sighed.

"Hank wanted more than I was willing to give him. He wanted to make love, but I wanted to wait until marriage. He cheated on me because he couldn't wait. He left me for someone who would put out. You...sorry, I mean guys I meet don't want to wait. If I don't put out, they head for the door."

"Wow. Why wait?"

Gina pressed her lips together for a second. "I've seen friends of mine hurt from relationships gone bad. I've seen scarred hearts or pregnancies change lives forever, and it was hard to watch...even harder to live."

"Obviously, I don't share that viewpoint, but for the past ten months I've lived a celibate life." He shook his head. "I think I've said too much." He gazed into Gina's eyes. *"Even harder to live,"* Sean recalled. *She'd been hurt before she met her ex. No wonder she's so careful not to be alone with a guy. She'd placed a lot of trust in me, having me sleep over the way she did.* "I understand. I wish I'd known about this so that I could've made things clear to Greg. Will you forgive me? I can't live without your friendship."

"I forgive you. I can't live without yours either. I was so sorry I chased you away. I heard your message. I didn't mean to hurt you. I was so angry."

He hugged her again. "It's okay," he whispered.

When Sean released her, he noticed a tear trickling down her cheek. He reached out to wipe it away, but she got to it first. He stopped his hand right before it touched her face although something drove him to keep going. Her lips formed a strained smile, and he found himself unable to stop staring at her mouth. His heart fluttered.

"I better head home," he said, standing in one motion.

"I know you won't sleep over, but you can always find a spare key in my secret spot outside my door."

"I remember."

"Also, would you like to come over for dinner sometime?"

"Sure. It's fine if Cindy comes too, right?"

"Yes, but you can come over even if she can't. I'll make sure Gene is here too. He moved nearby so we could watch out for each other more often."

"Cool. That'll be great. I'd like to hang out with him...her again."

"Don't stress. I can never see Gene as anything but a guy. He's always been my closest relative. It was hard when he lived three hours away. I'm glad he lives closer now."

"Just call me, and I'll tell Cindy."

"Okay."

He stopped short when he reached the door. Gina stood just inches away.

"I'm glad you didn't throw that away," he said, pointing at the bracelet.

"I told you I would never take it off. I meant that…no matter how angry I get at you."

"Thanks, that means a ton you saying that. Good night."

"Good night, Sean."

Sean grabbed and squeezed Gina's hand one last time before leaving her in the doorway, staring after him.

Chapter Eight

A couple weekends later, Gina called Sean to invite him and Cindy over for a restaurant style dinner. To her surprise, Cindy agreed to join Sean for the evening. Gina immediately called Gene to discuss the menu. She hoped to impress Cindy so she wouldn't have any reason to be suspicious.

However, when the night finally arrived and the doorbell rang, she opened the door to see only Sean standing in front of her with a bouquet of flowers.

"Sean, it's great to see you. No Cindy?"

Sean shook his head and handed over the bouquet. Gina smelled them and smiled.

"No, she had to work…again."

"Sorry."

"No worries. Am I good enough?"

"You're better than 'good enough'. Come on in." She opened the door wider to let him through.

"Wow. Food smells great."

"It's almost finished. Make yourself at home."

"Another family recipe?"

"Of course. Gene's mom's specialty. He's helping me prepare it."

"Can't wait," Sean said, smiling. He turned toward the iPhone she had set into a docking station. "What's playing? I don't know this one."

"It's Colbie Caillat."

"Never heard of her. Sounds like easy listening."

"Her songs are anything but easy. I'm convinced she sings about my life. I can relate to almost every song."

"What about the one she's singing now? 'Oxygen'? Can you identify with that one?"

Gina opened her mouth, panic stricken. She didn't want to lie, but she couldn't tell him the song reminded her of him either. *Why in the world did I play that song today of all days?*

"Cous', I need you," Gene called out, saving Gina from an awkward situation.

"I better go," she said, relieved.

"Sure," Sean agreed.

While transferring the pasta to the dining table, Gina caught a glimpse of Sean. Her heart pumped a little faster.

"What's got you so worked up, Sista?"

"He's listening to the lyrics. What if he realizes they're about him?" she whispered.

"Then perhaps we can see an end to your suffering, Cous'."

"What about Cindy's suffering?"

"Those are the breaks."

"You forget I know what that feels like. I don't want to cause that to happen to anyone."

"You need to stop trying to solve everyone else's problems. You can't help make everyone happy on this planet."

"No, not everyone, just Sean…and Cindy."

"Are you so sure he's happy?"

"Wha'…" Gina began, but then she noticed Sean closing in on them. She would have to ask Gene why he thinks Sean may not be happy.

****

Gene observed his cousin Gina's eyes sparkle every time Sean spoke to her about insignificant little details concerning the dinner or her time with the little ones at school. Gene was shocked that Sean could miss the extra color flowing through Gina's cheeks whenever he looked at her.

At least, Sean gobbled everything on his plate and even had seconds. Gene had worked feverishly to ensure everything was cooked to perfection for his favorite cousin. This meal would impress the greatest critic. Perhaps, it was for the best that Cindy didn't show up after all.

"So, Sean," Gene began, "why didn't Cindy come with you?"

"Gene!" Gina warned.

"It's all right, Gina," Sean said with a weird smile, almost sad. "She had to work, Gene."

"Does that happen often? Work taking up her time, I mean."

"I'd really hate to bore you with the details," Sean said.

"I'm all ears. I don't get bored easily. Go ahead. Tell us."

Before Sean could respond, Gene heard a swooshing sound from the laundry closet. Gina had placed one last load in the wash before Sean showed up, thinking to finish up her washing so she'd be free to go out the following day with some friends.

"Gina, do you hear that?" Gene asked.

"Hear what?"

Billiard Buddies

"It sounds like water in your closet."

Gina stood quickly almost throwing her chair over, but Sean caught it just in time. Gene followed Gina to discover water seeping under the closet door toward the carpeted living room area.

"Oh, no," Gina yelled and ran to the closet.

Opening the door allowed more water to escape, soaking Gina's new purple suede shoes Gene bought for his cousin only last week. He stood stiff in horror until Sean dashed toward Gina, almost knocking him over in a wake of gusty air.

"The hose broke!" Gina screamed, struggling with something behind the washer. "I'm not strong enough."

Sean pushed Gina—Gene thought too rough—out of the way and shoved his hand behind the washer as well. His black loafers were also getting soaked. Gene wished he could help, but there was no way he was getting his shoes wet. And exposing his feet was not an option. He hadn't had a pedicure in weeks. Gene wanted to encourage Sean to date his cousin, not run away in terror.

"Gina, my hand is too large to reach this valve without pulling the washer out. Is there another I can get to?"

"I'll go see," Gina said.

She ran frantically through the apartment, eyes wide, trying to locate the main shut off valve.

"Gina, talk to me!" Sean yelled, still fighting to squeeze his hand in too tiny a space.

"I can't find it," Gina answered frantically.

"Then come here and hold this hose so the water doesn't flow so much. *I'll* look for it."

Gina acquiesced, running to Sean's side. He quickly replaced his hand with Gina's before backing away, water spraying everywhere, soaking them before she got a firm hold.

Oh...my...goodness. Can things get any worse? Shut up! Don't even test fate by saying that, Gene thought.

"Where's your utility closet?" Sean asked.

"It's down the hall, but everybody on the floor shares it."

"We'll deal with the fallout later. I imagine I need a key."

"Yes. On the table by the front door," Gina answered, Sean already halfway to the key's location.

Sean rushed out the door. A minute later, the water stopped gushing. Soon afterward, Sean returned to Gina's side.

"You can let go now. I turned it off," he said, removing her hand from the hose.

Sean stared at Gina and his clothes. His laugher, so infectious, caused Gina and Gene to laugh as well.

"I can't believe how wet we got," Sean said.

With the spray from the hose, both Gina and Sean had gotten soaked from heads to twenty toes. Sean touched Gina's face, gently moving a wisp of wet hair out of her eyes. Without warning, Gina's laughter changed over into tears. She brushed Sean's hand away and ran toward her bedroom, crying.

Gene gasped. *I knew I was tempting fate. Now, it's worse.*

"What just happened here?" Sean said, perplexed, staring at Gene. "Should I go to her?"

"No. I'll go check on her. I'm sure she's just in shock." *Or just wishing you would plant one on her mouth.*

Gene knocked on Gina's door before entering.

"It's just me, sweetie," Gene said, but Gina's door wasn't locked when he turned the knob. He wouldn't be surprised if she really wished Sean had been the one bursting through her door. "How are you feeling?" he asked, settling next to Gina on her bed.

"I don't know. I'm afraid. I'm so afraid I'm not strong enough."

"Strong enough for what?"

"Strong enough to resist him. Whenever he holds me I wish he didn't have to let me go."

"Why won't you tell him how you feel?"

"No, I can't."

"Gina, there's a gorgeous man out there who just rescued you from drowning in your own apartment. I wish he were here for me, but he's here because of you. Why can't you see that?"

Gina wiped her cheeks and laughed hysterically. "I finally meet a beautiful man who's not interested in you and he belongs to someone else," Gina said, slamming her palms onto the bed covers.

Gene smiled and hugged her.

"What I am, I remember being all my life. But unless you rescue him from that ghastly girlfriend of his, he's sure to convert. Believe me, honey, his woman's bringing him down."

"How do you know this? He's never talked to you, and he hardly mentions her to me."

"*I* can tell. When he first shows up, he always looks like a lost puppy. But after a few minutes here, he's a new man. He comes alive when he's

with you. Besides, if *she* made him happy, he
wouldn't try so hard to avoid talking about her."

"Don't guys tend to talk about their lovers,
especially over drinks?"

"Your guy is a gentleman, Gina. I imagine he feels
uneasy over the little he's shared with you so far,
but he probably wishes he could tell you
everything because he's drawn to you. I just have
a sense about these things."

Gina shook her head vigorously. "I can't." She
cried again. "I can't do that, not even to her."

"All right. I'll let this go for now, but you have a
great guy out there with wet shoes. The least you
can do is dry him off."

Gina smiled then and kissed Gene on the cheek.
He grabbed some tissues to wipe her glistening
cheeks.

"Okay, *now* you can go take care of your guy."

"Stop, Gene. He's not my guy."

"Yet," he added.

Gina squinted at Gene before she left her
bedroom to check on Sean. When Gene and his
cousin reached the living room, they found Sean
on hand and knee, surrounded by towels. He
looked up and smiled. *He's a beautiful man, all
right.*

"You okay, Gina?" Sean asked.

"Yeah, I'll be okay. Thanks for doing this. I'm sorry you had to work after your special dinner."

"It's *our* special dinner, and I don't mind. I just hate seeing you so sad." He paused to squeeze out a wet towel over a bucket. "I called your superintendent. I found the number by the phone. Anyway, he's coming over to fix your hose."

"Thanks, Sean. Oh, um, I'm such a terrible host. Do you need a robe?"

"No, a towel is fine and then I'll head home."

Gina grabbed an extra towel and walked it over to Sean.

"Take it with you for the ride home. You can give it back to me later or not. Doesn't matter."

Sean accepted the towel and turned to Gene, who thought he just might faint.

"Thanks for the fabulous dinner. Perhaps, someday I can convince you to share that recipe."

"It's a family secret, but for you I may make an exception," Gene teased.

Sean leaned toward Gina and gave her a kiss on the cheek.

"Thanks for a great dinner experience. I don't remember the last time I laughed so hard. It felt great. I'm glad I was here for the flood."

Gina giggled.

"Thanks, Sean. Now go before you catch cold or something."

Sean smiled and backed away slowly. He seemed to have difficulty looking away from Gina. With his back up against the door, his sweet smile faded away seconds before he turned around to place a hand on the knob and slip quietly outside.

After Sean left, Gene turned to his cousin. "You are so crazy in love. I can't believe you haven't even noticed you soaked your suede shoes."

"Ooops," she said, and started to laugh.

Gene laughed too.

Chapter Nine

Cindy was ecstatic. She finally got what she'd been working so hard for. Sean had just placed the phone on the kitchen counter when Cindy burst through the door.

"I got it!" Cindy blurted out.

Sean looked at her, speechless with a questioning stare.

"I got the job in California." She rushed to Sean and wrapped her arms around his neck, kissing him all over his face.

"Whoa! That's great news, Cindy. When do you start?"

"Well, that's the thing. I start in less than two weeks."

"What?!" He unwrapped her arms and dropped them by her side. His glare unsettled her.

"You're still going with me, right? Because it would break my heart if you couldn't move when I did."

"Cindy, my job. They usually require two weeks' notice. I'll be giving them half that. I don't know."

"Please talk to your boss. This is so important to me."

Sean settled into a chair at the kitchen table. "Cindy, can't I meet you out there? I would only be a week behind your arrival."

She placed a hand on his shoulder. "Sean, you promised me you would leave when I did. I really need you there. I can't do this without you," she bemoaned, working her best pout with what she hoped were puppy-dog eyes.

Sean rolled his eyes, and Cindy's gut clenched. "All right. I'll talk to my boss tomorrow. Also, I'll be late coming home. I need to tell Gina about this."

Now it was her turn to roll eyes.

"Do you *really* have to see her? Can't you just tell her over the phone?" Cindy whined.

"No, Cindy. She's a close friend. She deserves to be told this in person."

Yeah, I wonder just how close you two have been.

Cindy sat across from Sean and asked solemnly, "Are you going to spend the night with her?"

"Of course not. I haven't since last year."

"Really?" Cindy asked, lightening up. "Why?" She hoped her tone came across as innocent curiosity.

"I didn't want to hurt you anymore. I just need some time to talk with her, explain things, that's all."

"Okay. I'm sorry. I just don't want to go without you."

"I know. I'll look into that."

"And I guess I'm worked up because she gave you that electronic toy."

"The Game Boy?"

"Yeah. I didn't even know you liked them. She seems to know a lot about you."

"We've had a lot of time to talk, but that's it. I'm your guy and I love you."

"But you hardly smile anymore," Cindy noted.

"It's tough to be happy when you cancel almost everything we plan together. I wanted so much for you to meet my friends and now we're moving."

"I'll do better at that. Once I get settled, our lives will go back to normal. You've been so patient. I'll make it up to you once we get out West."

Sean nodded and Cindy kissed him appreciatively.

****

Monday had been a challenging day for Sean. First, he spent an hour explaining to his boss why he would be leaving in a week. Mr. Shriver was furious, but fortunately understood Sean's predicament. Sean agreed to remain available via cell phone and email until someone else could take over his accounts.

Next, Sean contacted Pete about holding onto Sean's car until it could be shipped out to California. Of course, Pete was shocked about the sudden move, but he was a great sport, as always.

Lastly, and he did not look forward to this, Sean knew he needed to face someone for whom he cared deeply to explain why he wouldn't be around any longer. He felt a deep pain in his chest but had trouble figuring out why the idea of leaving hurt so much.

He had met the one person who challenged him in a game he loved to play. A well matched opponent, Gina didn't lose games on purpose to steal his sympathy. He could be real with her. He could relax around her and dance.

Sean also liked her independent nature. How many times had he offered to walk her home before she accepted his company without a rebuttal? He smiled at that thought. He'd also come to enjoy her presence when Cindy was too busy to keep her promises. He had become emotionally linked to Gina and now he had to say good-bye.

No, he couldn't say "so long" over the phone. She meant too much to him in a way Cindy could never understand. He had to catch Gina at home so he could talk to her. After Sean got off from work, he called Gina's home phone from his car.

****

Gina had had a great day. She and Sean were on great terms again. The school day went without a hitch. The children did their assignments and behaved well. Today was super.

Having run some errands after work, Gina arrived home much later than usual. She entered her apartment and dropped her purse and keys on their usual spot, the table near the front door. She checked the answering machine and noticed a solid green light – no messages.

Just as she turned away to head for her bedroom, the house phone rang. Gina glanced at caller id and recognized Sean's cell phone number. Great! Her crazy flood of tears hadn't scared him away. She smiled as she answered the phone.

"Hello, friend," she answered cheerfully.

"Hi, Gina. Are you going to be home for a while? I need to come over and talk to you."

"Yes. Is everything all right?" Gina asked, having detected the tension in his voice.

"I'll tell you everything when I get there," he replied. "I'm leaving work now. I'll be there soon."

Billiard Buddies

Gina did not like the sound of Sean's voice. She racked her brain wondering what could be wrong. She walked over to the sofa to sit and exhaled loudly. She would lose her mind if he figured out what the song "Oxygen" really meant to her...that he was *her* oxygen in so many ways. After a few minutes, Gina stood and scrutinized her apartment's appearance. She tidied up a bit and steadied herself for his visit.

Sean arrived, his eyes somber with his lips pressed in a line. Gina stared at him as he grasped her hand and led her back to the sofa where she'd spent too much time mulling over what this talk would entail. Her legs froze when he settled into the pillows.

I'm so scared right now. What could have him so worked up? I'm usually the emotional one.

"Please sit," Sean requested, tugging her arm down toward him.

Gina obliged.

****

Why does this hurt so much? "Gina, Cindy got a job offer and she's going to take it."

"That's good, isn't it?"

Gina drew her hand to her chest when he shook his head.

"It's in California. I'm moving there with her."

Gina looked away briefly. When she faced him again, her eyes glistened like glass.

"When?"

"This weekend," he replied, taking her hand again into his, but she pulled her hand away.

"When did you find out about this?"

"Last night. I would have called, but I thought it would be better to tell you in person."

He reached out for her hand again, but Gina eased away and got up.

"Don't touch me. How long have you known?"

Her words stung him like they had every other time she shut him out when the hurt overflowed.

"I just found out, Gina."

"That's *not* what I mean. How long have you known about California?"

Sean sighed and stood, facing her.

"I knew at Christmas. She flew out for an interview then."

"You knew when you stayed here the day after Christmas and didn't say anything? Why didn't you tell me? Why wait until now?" Her voice started cracking.

"I didn't want you to worry just in case she never got the job. I was hoping she wouldn't get it." *Oh, gosh, Gina, please don't cry.*

"Sean, why? You're one of my closest friends. Why would you keep this from me?"

Sean felt the urge to hold Gina to help make this situation better somehow and reached out to her.

"Don't touch me!" she said, waving her hands wildly to keep him at bay. "Don't touch me." Her voice cracked and tears streamed down her cheeks.

Sean swallowed hard when a spasm hammered his gut. *Why did the move have to be now? I don't know how to fix this.* "What can I do to make this better?" he asked.

Stay, she seemed to beg with her eyes, but instead said, "Perhaps, you should leave now."

"Gina, I don't want to leave you like this." Sean clutched at his chest, the pain growing unbearably intense. Why did he feel this way? "Please, don't push me away. I need you. Let me hold you."

"I can't." She took a step back. "Please go, Sean."

I'm about to lose it in front of her. This really hurts. This really stinks. "I'll call you later. Please answer, okay?"

"I will. I promise. Just go. I wish you well on your new life in California with Cindy. I do…but I need you to leave."

Sean contemplated Gina with a doleful heart. His feet didn't want to move, but he willed them to do so. As he walked sluggishly down the steps, he clutched at his shirt. *Why does it hurt so much? I don't really want to leave.*

****

Sean went home to an excited and energetic Cindy. She had already started packing clothes. Many boxes were stacked high in the living room with packing tape lying on the coffee table.

"Hi, honey, I wanted to get started. We have to get packed by the end of the week. The movers will be arriving late Friday afternoon. Your suitcases are near the closet."

Sean glanced around the room. Everything seemed to spin around him.

"I'm gonna sit for a while. I'll start packing later."

Sean plopped down on the sofa and stared at the phone in his hands. He wanted to call Gina, but he knew it would be too soon. She would still be upset that he hadn't told her about the possibility of his moving sooner. He wasn't sure why he hadn't told her, but he felt horrible that Gina felt betrayed.

Cindy joined him and snuggled close. "Isn't it exciting, Sean? We're going to California." She gave him a quick kiss and hurried back to her packing.

Sean huffed. All he could think about was his friendship with Gina and the dejected look in her eyes.

For the rest of the week, Sean devoted his energies to helping Cindy pack. However, during one packing break each day, he made a phone call to Gina to check in on her. His best friend still seemed pretty down, but at least she answered the phone whenever he called. Otherwise, he'd have to break her door down if she removed the key from its hidden location. He blinked, hardly believing he entertained such thoughts.

Two days before he and Cindy were scheduled to leave, Sean called Gina after sealing the last box.

I just need to hear the sound of your voice.

****

Gina replayed Sean's last visit in her mind. He tried to hold her hand. When she had pulled away and started crying, he attempted to embrace her.

"Let me hold you," he had said.

She recalled her exact thoughts when he said those words to her.

You have no idea how much I need you too. If I let you hold me, I won't let go, not this time.

So she chased Sean away. He made her promise to answer when he called, but she thought she'd pushed him away for the last time. She never expected to hear from him again. Perhaps it was better that way.

However, Sean did call and she picked up the phone to hear his wonderful, sweet voice. That's how it would be from now on. She wouldn't see him all the way in California. They'd spend their free time discussing difficult pool shots over the phone. Competing with the other guys would never be as thrilling. But Sean meant more to her than a well matched sparring partner. She had fallen in love with him.

The phone rang, interrupting her thoughts. She stared at the calendar while she picked up the phone.

Two days before he leaves me...forever.

"Hey. How are you?" Sean asked.

"Okay, I guess. How's the packing going?"

"I just finished the last box. The movers are coming tomorrow."

Gina squeezed her eyes shut. She felt like crying, but tried her best to control her voice. "That's great," she said, her voice quivering slightly.

"Oh, Gina, I wish this were easier. I feel really bad about how quickly this is all happening."

She could never fake anything with Sean. He always knew her true feelings even though she had grown effective in hiding their causes.

"I better go now. It's late."

"Gina, please talk to me a little longer." His pleading chipped away at the emotional wall she struggled daily to patch up.

"I really must go."

"Can I call you tomorrow?"

"Um, no, it's probably better if I just see you on Saturday. It's been hard talking to you every night."

"I...I...we'll see you Saturday morning. Good night, Gina."

"Good night, Sean."

Gina clicked the end call button and let the phone thump onto the counter. She peered around her apartment and found she could hardly breathe. She needed oxygen. She needed him.

She'd hardly allowed pain to get to her, but Sean had unplugged her bottle of pent up sorrow. His gentle nature had coaxed her heart to let him in, and now she would never experience the joy that should come when that happens.

Gina's inability to avoid another broken heart angered her. Sean shouldn't be blamed. He'd remained faithful to his lover and yet had remained a conscientious friend.

Why can't that be enough for me? And why am I so freaked out that he's leaving me? I've got to control these crazy emotions.

Seemingly non-ending tears dropped from her chin. Unable to see clearly, Gina sank to the floor and continued to weep bitterly. After a few minutes, she stood and wiped at her eyes so she could grab her phone. Gina dialed a familiar number and croaked, "Joanna? He's leaving," before succumbing to overwhelming sorrow once more.

Chapter Ten

Gina dreaded this day, the day her friend Sean would leave her forever. Sean told her he'd call often, that he'd visit once in a while, but Gina knew only too well Cindy would never let that happen. Although she'd never met Sean's girlfriend, she knew distance would successfully diminish her friendship with Sean.

The last few days had been quite emotional. Gina never remembered crying so much, not even when Hank cheated on her. Why in the world did Sean mean so much to her? He'd never so much as tried to kiss her, for which she remained grateful. She'd be more torn up now. No, it was best he move away before she did what she hated. She'd remain strong and let Sean go with Cindy far, far away. She wondered if New York would miss his presence as much as she remained sure she would.

It was nine o'clock and Sean would be arriving soon with his girlfriend. *I don't know if I even want to meet her. What if she thinks I'm trying to steal him when I've done all I can not to?* Gina sighed when the buzzer sounded from the main front door. She pushed a button to let them in.

****

"Are you sure she even wants to meet me?" Cindy challenged.

"I know you've been hesitant about meeting Gina, but I need you two to meet each other. It's way overdue." Cindy followed his eyes as he looked up to see Gina waiting for them in her doorway. "Hey, friend."

"Hi, Sean. This must be Cindy." Gina's tone seemed sweet…too sweet.

Sean nodded and presented Cindy to Gina, the girl whose very existence threatened to shake everything up.

"It's good to meet you, Cindy," Gina said, offering her hand.

Cindy took her hand and shook it. "It's good to meet you too, Gina. Sean is always talking about your billiard competitions. He says you're very good."

Gina folded her arms. "Yes, I love the game."
Gina gazed affectionately at Sean and smiled with perfectly full, pouty lips.

Cindy forced a counter-smile, but took note of the way Gina continued to gaze at her boyfriend. *How could he claim he's never even kissed her?*
"Sean, we better go. At this rate, we'll make it just in time."

"I'm aware of how much time we have. I need a few moments," Sean snapped.

"Don't be too long." Cindy started walking down the stairs, but stopped after four steps. "Bye, Gina," she said, turning half-way around to keep Sean in her sight. *I'm so glad I'm getting him away from you.*

"Bye, Cindy." Gina turned her attention to Sean. "I'm going to miss you, Sean."

Sean grasped Gina's hands and held them securely in his own.

Cindy wished she could see the way Sean looked at Gina and grew uneasy at seeing how much the pending separation had affected him. *I feel like I've already lost your heart.*

****

Gina's hands shivered in his.

"I'm going to miss you too," Sean began, barely above a whisper. "In fact, I miss you already. I guess we'll have to wait a while longer to determine who'll be the pool champion."

"I suppose," Gina said, her eyes avoiding his at first, probably because Cindy only stood a few feet away.

"I meant what I said about visiting each other. I want you to come visit us out West, okay?"

"I don't think that would work, Sean. Cindy, well, she's suspicious of me."

"How can you tell that from one meeting?"

"It's the way she looked at me. I think this is good-bye," Gina whispered.

Sean felt a pang in his chest when she said "good-bye".

"I don't want it to be good-bye, Gina. Please don't end this here, now."

"I don't want to, but…"

"No, don't say it." Sean drew Gina close and gave her a hug.

Gina buried her head in Sean's chest and wet his shirt with a few tears.

"Sean, we need to go," Cindy growled.

"Okay, I'm coming." Sean released Gina and gazed fondly at her moist face. "I'm sorry, Gina. I need to go." He kissed her on the forehead.

"Okay," Gina replied, nodding. "Have a safe trip." She quickly wiped tears off her cheeks.

"Thanks. I'll call you." Sean stepped away, but everything in his body yearned to stay. He clutched at his aching chest as he glanced back at her. Tears began to well up on his lids. *What am I doing?*

"Sean, hurry, please. We'll be late," Cindy pressed.

Sean pulled his eyes away from Gina and followed Cindy out the door.

****

Gina cried, her heart breaking, as she saw Sean leave. *I love you so much. Oh, God, I don't know if I'm going to make it without you.* She stooped down to get the spare key from under the mat. She had left it there after Sean returned it, hoping he would make use of it again. Gina turned the key around between her fingers, knowing that he wouldn't need it anymore. She entered her apartment, closed the door, and slumped to the floor, tears dripping onto the carpet. After a few minutes, Gina called her cousin.

"He's gone, Gene. I need you to come over."

"Sweetie, I'm held up right now, but I'll come over tonight. Hang in there, baby. I'll bring over some ice cream."

"I'll try," Gina said, winded. "Come as quickly as you can. I feel weak and I need to be around someone I trust." Hanging up, she crawled to the far side of the apartment and sat under the window where she wept.

Whoever said "parting is such sweet sorrow"? No way is it "sweet". All I feel is an ocean of regret. I never even said "I love you" to him. Now he's gone. I won't ever have that chance again.

Gina continued to sit under the window even when she heard Sean's voice on the answering machine during his many attempts to reach her. She felt somewhat guilty for not answering. She knew he hated when she pulled away. She hugged herself and cried some more, hoping Sean would stop calling. However, he didn't. His persistence continued for over two hours to both phones with the most recent call made to her cell. Gina finally answered her phone, but found Sean had hung up.

Why is he still calling? He should be on the plane by now. I hope they're okay.

A noise startled Gina, and she stared at her door.

I think I forgot to lock the door. I hope that's not Hank. I can't deal with him now, not like this.

****

Sean and Cindy got into the taxi. He held onto his phone tightly as he glanced back at the apartment building he had visited so many times before.

On the way to the airport, Sean called Gina's cell. He hoped she'd answer. He so wanted to hear her voice again. Disappointed, he placed the phone in his pocket.

He barely noticed the multitude of yellow cabs racing to their various destinations. He stared at the bigger than life billboards, but what they advertised didn't matter much. He hardly cared that one belonged to Cindy. His mind kept going back to the great matches he played and the cute face on the other side of the studded cue. He missed that face although it had only been a few minutes since he laid eyes on it.

After getting to the airport, Sean and Cindy checked in and went through the security check. He reluctantly dropped his cell along with his keys into the square tub. He stepped through the metal detector while straining his ears to hear whether his phone rang. But it didn't, not even after the long stroll down the hall past tiny shops selling snacks and entertainment magazines.

When they found a place to sit, Sean called Gina's home phone. She still did not answer, so he left a message.

"Gina, I need you to answer the phone so I know you're okay. Please answer the phone. I'm at the airport now, so you can still call me before I board. Shoot." He hung up the phone, dropping it on his lap, and bent over, elbows bored into his knees and his face buried in his hands. *Gina, I just want to hear you one more time.* Sean stood, agitated. He picked up his phone that had fallen onto the floor. Cindy's frown turned into a weak smile. He needed some space. "You want a drink? I'm gonna take a walk."

"Sure, a latte would be great."

Sean walked down the hallway and stopped temporarily to lean against the wall. He didn't know how to describe what he was experiencing. He only knew he would miss having Gina in his life. He didn't want to admit she was right, that he wouldn't be able to see her or talk to her as he wanted. He wanted to believe Cindy wouldn't mind so much when she had him all to herself, but he doubted she'd care much about anything but her new job.

After he got moving again, he went to the restroom and washed his face before heading to the café to buy two lattes. When he returned to Cindy, he handed her a latte and sat down.

"Thanks," she said, coldly.

Sean took a sip of his latte and stared into the crowd.

"Why are you so worked up over her? Did you *sleep* with her?"

"Cindy, I told you I *didn't* touch her. I have never thought of her that way. Gina is one of my best friends, and I miss her a lot. Why do you think I did?" Sean said, slightly annoyed.

"Didn't you see the way she looked at you?"

"What're you talking about? She's sad I'm leaving."

"That's not what I meant. When she looked at you this morning, well, I could tell she's in love with you."

"What? How could you know that?"

"She never told you? I guess she is a better woman than I thought. I would steal you the first chance I got." Cindy shuffled in her seat. "So, do you love her?" she said with strained tenderness.

"I love her as a friend."

"I think it's more serious than that. The way you're brooding over her—like a lovesick puppy. How could you sit there and not realize how you feel about her?"

Is that why it hurts so much? Could I be in love with Gina? He turned his head to gaze into her eyes. "Cindy, when we go to California, is this relationship going anywhere? Would you be ready to marry me?"

"Sean." Cindy laughed nervously. "I told you we would talk about that when we got out there, after we're settled in. You know I'm crazy about you."

After setting his latte under his seat, Sean knelt on both knees in front of Cindy. "I need to know now. I feel like you're married to your job and that if we got married, I'd be married to your job too. I can't do that, Cindy."

Cindy's eyes welled up. "Sean, please don't decide this now. Let's figure this out later. Please."

He wondered why her tears didn't affect him.

"I need to call Gina again. I'm worried about her. She hasn't answered any of my calls."

Sean stood and sauntered away to make the call. Once again, he left a message, but Gina did not pick up. He knew she had to be there. She wouldn't leave the apartment after crying the way she did before he left her.

He wanted to hear her voice. He wanted to ask her something. He wanted...he wouldn't say, not even to himself. He hung up.

After another hour, the airline was ready to board passengers. Sean and Cindy gathered their things and filed into the crowded line. He shifted from one foot to the other as they waited to board the plane.

"What's keeping them so long?" Cindy asked, stamping her foot.

Sean stared at his shoes and then at the back of Cindy's head. "Cindy, I can't go...I can't go with you."

Cindy quickly turned to face him. "Sean, no. Think about this," she begged.

"I have. There's so much that didn't make sense. I…I've been racking my brain…trying to figure out…why I miss her so much, why it hurts. You're right, I *am* in love with her. I can't believe I didn't realize this. I guess I was trying so hard to, um, stay loyal to you. I ignored my feelings, ignored all the signs."

"Sean," Cindy said, grabbing his arm. "We can talk about this when we get to our new place. I promise things will be different. It's been hard ever since the cancer, but I'm getting there."

"I know it's been tough for you, first thinking you were pregnant, and then realizing you had a cluster of cancer cells inside you. That whole thing affected you, no doubt, but you've always been driven by your work. There's no room for me in your life. There's no room for kids in your life and I want them."

"I'm sure someday I'll be able to have kids."

"Yes, but you don't really want them, and I don't want you to have them just because I do. That wouldn't be right or fair to them." He paused to wipe the tears on her cheek. "I'm suddenly realizing how much she's meant to me and I need to find out if she feels the same way. I'm gonna go over to her place now." He retrieved his wallet from a pant pocket.

"Sean."

He pulled some bills out of his wallet. "Here's some cash to mail my stuff back. Just throw everything in a box. And I'll send you more to return my stuff that's being delivered."

"Sean, you're being rash. Come with me. We can sort everything out."

Passengers started walking past them onto the plane. Cindy became frantic, pleading with Sean to stay with her.

"Even if I went with you, it wouldn't work out between us. We don't know each other anymore. We don't talk. We don't enjoy each other. I don't know what I'm hanging on to except familiarity."

"I could be wrong about how she feels."

"Even so, I need her friendship. Every step I take toward that plane hurts even more. Even if she never loves me like you said, my heart will be happy just to be around her. She makes me laugh. She values me and what I think."

"Gosh, Sean, I'm so sorry."

"The sad part is, I still love you, but I'm okay with letting you go. I can't live without Gina." Sean kissed Cindy gently on her quivering lips. "Bye, Cindy. Have a safe trip." Sean took one last congenial look at Cindy before turning and walking away with his backpack and duffle bag.

He imagined Cindy standing in place staring at him walk away, hoping he'd turn around and take her in his arms, but he just kept on walking. When she lost sight of him, she would board the plane knowing she lost him. She'd have to live with the thought that she got her career and lost her man. However, no matter what, he would have gained the opportunity to be with the best friend he ever had.

Chapter Eleven

Sean called Gina again and again when he left the airport in a taxi he'd flagged down. Gina never answered. *Please be okay.* Sean grew agitated as he thought about the possibility of Gina drowning her sorrows with a bottle like she'd done before. He shook the thought from his mind.

Sean paid the taxi and hurried to the front door. *If she's not answering the phone, how will I get in?* Then Sean remembered something. He searched his pant pockets and found the key for the main door. In all his distress during the departure, he forgot to return the key to Gina and hadn't paid attention when he emptied his pockets at the airport. *Perhaps, it was fate.*

He struggled up the steps with his bags and stood at the door, dialing her cell phone this time. He listened to her phone ring a few times on the other side of the door. He hung up and checked under the mat to discover the key had been removed.

In a desperate attempt, Sean tried the door knob. *If it's locked, I'll break in.* However, when he turned the knob, the door opened easily.

He observed Gina, silhouetted by the light streaming through the window under which she sat, surrounded by mounds of tissues.

Has she been crying all this time?

At the sight of him, Gina dropped the cell phone on the carpet near her thigh and stared at him, mouth and eyes opened wide.

"Oh, Gina, why didn't you answer? I've been calling you for hours."

"I was crying. I didn't want you to worry. Why are you here?" She fumbled, awkwardly grabbing used tissues, stuffing them back into a box.

Ignoring her question for the moment, Sean continued, "I thought something bad happened. That you might have..." He trailed off, unable to say the words. He closed the door behind him without taking his eyes off her.

"You thought I hurt myself. I'm not depressed enough to do that. I just missed you a ton."

Dropping his bags on the floor, he added, "I needed to know if you were okay. I needed to see you. At the airport, I realized something. I realized I didn't want to leave...you." He stepped closer to her as he spoke.

Gina placed her hand over her heart and continued to stare at him with what he guessed were hopeful eyes.

"I realized something else." Sean paused and held his hands out to Gina. "I'm in love with you, and I can't live without you in my life."

At those words, Gina stood quickly and rushed toward Sean as if he said something she longed to hear. He held her face in his hands and began kissing her with all the passion and desire that had been repressed over the past months. Her lips, so soft and warm, moved against his with similar intensity.

She also held his face in her hands as if allowing herself to be engulfed by his emotive expression of yearning for her. Sean stopped and gazed into her eyes.

"I'll wait for you," he promised, hoping she understood what he meant.

Gina's smile confirmed that she did. She embraced him and nestled her head onto his chest.

"You came back for me. I love you so much."

"Why didn't you tell me how you felt? I had no idea," he said. "Cindy told me while we waited for the plane."

Gina eased away and peered at him, confused. "She knew?"

"She said it was the way you looked at me when you said 'good-bye'. I totally missed it. I'm so sorry I did. I wish you told me."

"I didn't tell you because I didn't want to be responsible for splitting you up. I didn't want to be the other woman. I didn't want to hurt her like I was hurt."

"Oh, Gina, you're the best. Mmm." He squeezed her and grinned. "You're my best friend. It hurt so much to leave you. I couldn't leave."

"Why didn't *you* say something?"

"I guess I didn't want to admit I fell for you. I wanted you to stay close. I didn't want to be without you in my life. I only realized what that meant when I sat in the airport. I had to come back to you."

"What about Cindy?"

"It's over. She left. I told her to send my stuff back. We existed in the same space, but our hearts had been separated long before. I invested a lot into the relationship, so I didn't want to let go." Sean paused briefly. "But I did that today." He touched Gina's face. "I want *you*."

"Where do we go from here? Do you still love her?"

Sean knew he couldn't lie to himself, and definitely refused to lie to his best friend. "That's the tricky part. I do still love her, but I'm in love with you. You fit me like a glove. She was more like a mitten. However, I need some time to get over her before I can consider you my girlfriend. I hope that's okay."

"I understand," she said, pausing. "I figured as much. Please don't rush through your feelings." Gina smiled. "I'm not going anywhere."

They kissed again. Sean lost himself when his lips touched hers. He wrapped his arms around her waist, pulling her close. After what seemed like eternity, Gina pulled away and gasped.

"Oh, gosh, I just realized you don't have anywhere to stay."

Sean smiled. "Yeah. I'm homeless and only have the clothes in my bags. I'll stay in a hotel until I find a place."

"Stay here."

"I couldn't, Gina. Not alone, not with the way I feel about you now."

"I'll call Gene. If he can come over, would you consider staying here?"

A familiar calm spread over Sean's heart. He'd come home to Gina.

"Yes, I would. I'd like to."

****

Gina phoned Gene, her heart fluttering with excitement.

"Hey, Cous', are you okay?" Gene asked.

"I'm better than okay," Gina said jovially. "He came back. He didn't go to California."

"Wow. Really? He must be in love with you. I knew everything would work out."

"Sure, you did. I need a favor."

"What is it, sweetie?"

"Can you stay over for a few days starting tonight? Sean doesn't have a place to stay, and we don't want to be alone."

"I have a date tonight."

"Come after the date, then."

"We were planning a slumber party."

"Well, postpone it. You know how I feel about your...activities."

"I know. You hate the sin, not the sinner," Gene commented nonchalantly.

"I've never said that. I just know you won't be able to keep your hands off him, and I don't want anything going on in my apartment," Gina retorted.

Gene sighed. "Only because I love you, Gina. I'll be there."

Gina sent kisses over the phone. "Thanks, Gene. Thank you so much."

"I'll be late, but I should be there by eleven tonight. Tell him to keep his hands off you, okay?"

"I will." Gina hung up the phone and smiled at Sean. "He'll come. So will you stay?"

"I'll stay," Sean responded. "How about something to eat? I'm hungry. Did you even eat after I left?"

"No, I completely missed lunch."

"Let's go out. I've wanted to treat you to dinner for some time, but it didn't seem right. Here's our chance."

"Okay, I'll change. How should I dress?"

"Nice, casual. It'll be a sit down dinner with wine."

"We're not going to get drunk anymore, are we?"

"No, I think I'll stay sober from here on out. I think I drank because I was so unhappy with Cindy. I'm not unhappy with you. Even when you frustrate me, like when you don't answer your phone, I'm not driven to drink."

"Bad habit. I'll work on that. I know how much it hurts you. I don't want you to be sad anymore, not like you've been."

"Thanks, Gina." He pecked her on the lips and smiled. "Now go get changed."

"Be right back."

Gina quickly put on a simple halter top flower dress. Sean beamed when he saw her walk toward him.

"Will this do?" she asked.

"It's perfect. You're perfect."

"What's perfect? Tell me."

Sean grinned. "The way it hugs your curves." He reached out and slid his hand around her waist. "And your shoulders…your face…so beautiful…and radiant…your lips. I want to kiss you again."

She hardly said, "Please," before his lips pressed against hers once more. He pulled away too quickly.

"We better go."

"I know."

After they left the apartment holding hands, Sean hailed a taxi which drove them to an Applebee's restaurant downtown. The maître d' offered a table with two chairs in the center of the crowded room, but Sean requested a booth in the corner off to the side for a little more privacy since no one sat in the adjoining booth.

"What would you like to drink?" asked the waitress.

"Red Wine, please" Gina answered.

"I should have known," he said, grinning at her. Then, he faced the waitress and added, "Make that two."

Gina waited until the young woman strolled away. "What did you mean?"

"It's my favorite wine too."

Grasping both hands, Sean intertwined their fingers. He let go when the waitress returned with their drinks and took their order.

Gina gazed into Sean's eyes as they waited for the waitress to serve dinner. His arm extended across the table, palm upward, inviting her to rest hers within his grasp.

"Wow. It's weird this being our first official date. I feel like I already know you," Sean said.

"There *are* some things you don't know yet."

"That's true," he said thoughtfully, stroking the back of her hand. "Hmm. Where should I begin?" He paused. "I know. Why didn't you ever hook up with one of the guys? At one point or another, all of them have flirted with you. Why did you fall for me?"

"Well, first of all they all drank way too much."

"Have you forgotten how I ended up in your apartment?" He smirked.

"You stopped at the first sign of being tipsy. The rest of them didn't know when to say 'when'."

"You've got a point," Sean admitted.

"They were spoiling you. I always hoped you'd stop hanging with them, but then I wouldn't see you as much," Gina said.

"I see."

"As for why I fell for you, well, you were a perfect gentleman whenever we spoke or danced. You were faithful to Cindy although I sensed there was some tension. You are everything I dreamed of in a guy for me, but to have you meant I'd be destroying some of the things I admired most. So I settled. I didn't want to lose the special friendship we had."

"You realize, Gina, we still have that." He drew her hand to his lips and locked her gaze.

His touch sent shivers up her arm. She fought for composure. "Yes," she agreed, nodding, "and now, much more."

Only when the waitress returned with the entrees did Sean release her hand. No matter when she glanced up from her food, Sean always caught her gaze. Even though he seemed less interested in his dinner than with her, he finished first.

"Too far away," he said, and before she blinked twice, he'd scooted next to her. She shuffled over to give him room when their arms brushed against each other. She enjoyed the cozy warmth of his skin, so much so, she stopped eating and placed her fork on the dish. "Are you finished?"

"I think so."

"Would you like dessert?"

"No, I'm good," she replied, leaning into him.

Sean nuzzled her ear, his warm breath tickling the hairs on her cheek. Gina's skin grew warm. He eased away…barely, studying her.

"If we played pool tonight, you'd lose," he said in a soft and lascivious tone.

She dared peer up into his face that held a hue like hers felt. "So would you," she whispered back. Then, he gifted her with a deep throaty chuckle. The kind that'd buckle her knees if she were on her feet. Her abdomen quivered. Gosh, he was so close.

"That's my girl. I knew you were still in there. I want all of you to be present tonight."

His lips, soft and warm, tasted sweet. Her pulse quickened. She only remembered they were in a restaurant when the maître d' seated someone in the adjoining booth. Sean eased away, much slower than before, sending shivers down her spine.

"You realize the date's not over yet," he whispered into her ear.

"What do you have in mind?" She trembled when his thigh brushed her own.

"Something where there're people, but a little more intimate. No tables."

She glanced up at him only to be greeted with a flirtatious wink. Perhaps, she should have that dessert after all.

****

The need to be close to Gina overwhelmed him, so he slid into the booth next to her. Sean leaned closer and sniffed Gina, taking in the scent of flowers carried along on a summer breeze. He couldn't bear being more than a few inches away from her, this woman he'd finally allowed himself to explore. He pressed his back to the cushion when the waitress returned.

"Would you like dessert?" she asked.

He gazed at Gina whose skin shone like a dew-bathed rose.

"Yes, I would."

"Do you mind sharing?" he asked Gina. Not that he couldn't afford his own. Man, he'd buy her the whole lot so she'd stay up with him all night. He didn't want to sleep and miss even one moment with her. Instead, he longed to share something with her. Deep down, he always did. Now, he finally had the opportunity.

"No, I don't mind. Do you have a preference?"

"Pick anything you want."

Gina turned toward the waitress. "Cheesecake, please."

"My favorite. Two spoons," he said, even though he figured they'd only use one.

Sean watched the waitress walk away. He wondered why it'd hurt so much when he decided to leave for California. Even when he'd resolved to just being Gina's friend, he longed to be near her to play, to eat, and to talk. He didn't realize until almost too late the hold she had on him. He'd never leave her again. Never want to be on a business trip for more than a day. Never want to wake up unable to see her face first. He had come home to her. Gina was his home and his heart.

He liked her fierce energy during a fight and looked forward to making up with her after each and every one. Now, he could finally let himself indulge in her engaging personality and contemplate the way she licked cheesecake off her upper lip.

With patrons now in the booth behind them, the restaurant suddenly felt crowded. He needed more intimacy. He'd waited so long.

****

After Sean and Gina finished dinner, they went to a movie to pass the time. Sean grinned at Gina's excitement to see the latest romantic movie with a touch of adventure in the theatres. There would be no need to cry when this one ended, at least not sad tears. Seating remained plentiful in the stadium theatre. Privacy would not be a problem.

"What's your preference? Back? Middle?" Sean asked.

"You choose this time."

"All right. Let's go way in back. I'd like to have you to myself,"

Sean stole quick moments to kiss her throughout the movie. Gina's heart melted every time he stroked her cheek.

The ease with which her heart opened to Sean frightened her. She'd wanted this…him for so long and now that she'd finally received such a great gift, thoughts of losing Sean plagued her. She had no reason to worry. He'd assured her he had come to her and left his life with Cindy behind.

145

But, what if Cindy was pregnant? Would obligation draw him away? But no, he'd mentioned once he and Cindy hadn't been intimate in months.

Oh, why can't I let this go?

Gina knew why. The painful betrayals and encounters she'd experienced soiled her view of men...her trust in them. Then, Sean came along and gave her hope. His friendship, deep care, and unconditional love wowed her from the first night they met. And he was a great pool player, the only one with the mad skills to best her. The only one she could not avoid falling in love with.

His nose brushing against her ear pulled Gina out of those miserable memories. She closed her eyes. His kisses made her feel things...everywhere. Tightening her grip on his hand didn't help. Her breathing came out in short gasps. She didn't want him to stop, but if he didn't, she would absolutely embarrass herself in the theatre.

****

Halfway through the movie, Sean nuzzled Gina's ear. She leaned into him. He brushed six quick kisses on her cheek while her grasp tightened around his fingers.

"Do you want me to stop?"

"No. But I need you to. Please. I can't..." She moaned quietly.

Sean chuckled softly. "I love making you blush."

"That's not the only thing you're making me do," she admitted in a sultry tone.

"Okay, I'll behave," he said with one more peck on her cheek before settling back in his seat, resigned to watching the rest of the film which was actually quite good. He laughed once, maybe twice.

Underlying heartache gnawed at him. Although he now had Gina, ending things with Cindy the way he did still left him in limbo. He needed time for a clean break before taking things with Gina further.

Sean brought Gina's hand to his cheek. A pang clenched his gut at the thought he would have been on a plane to California at that moment. No, he'd without a doubt, made the right choice. No doubt, he'd have been on the first plane back. Gina called to his heart. She always had, especially when they battled around the pool table.

He loved her with everything he had.

Sean hadn't realized how much he craved closeness and intimacy where what he offered was reciprocated. He kissed Gina's cheek again, and with her leaning into the kiss it filled him with overwhelming gratitude.

He'd found his "one."

****

By the time they returned to Gina's apartment, Gene was there waiting for them. Sean slept on the sofa while Gina gave her cousin the play by play of the evening in her room. Gene refused to let her sleep until she'd told him the way she felt when Sean had given her that spicy good-night kiss.

"I am so happy for you, Gina. You two will be good together."

"He still loves her, though. What if he misses her too much?"

"I don't think you need worry about that. He just needs a little time, but you're the one he'll stay with in the end."

"I hope you're right. I love him with all my heart."

"If he asked you to marry him, would you?" Gene asked.

"I think if he were to ask me tonight, I would say 'yes'. For now though, that's only a dream."

"Sweet dreams, Cous'. You deserve them."

"You too, Gene. Thanks for sleeping over."

Gina yawned in response to her cousin's sigh. She exhaled and smiled as she thought about Sean. Soon, she drifted off to sleep.

Chapter Twelve

Gina woke up early Sunday morning to find Sean in the kitchen cooking breakfast. She felt warm all over just seeing him standing there.

"Sean, you didn't have to do this!"

"Good morning," he said, smiling. "You've always been the chef. I wanted to do this for you. Have a seat," he continued, gesturing toward a chair. "It's my turn to serve you."

"Are you for real?"

"Kiss me just to make sure. I think I may be dreaming, that I may not be staring at the woman I'm nuts about."

Sean leaned toward Gina and pressed his lips against hers. Her heart fluttered wildly.

"Good," he said. "You're real. It would be a drag to wake up and have to come find you all over again."

Gina grinned.

"So, Sean, what's for breakfast?"

"No secret recipe here. Eggs and sausage. Hope you like it." Sean placed a plate of food in front of Gina and poured coffee into a cup for her.

Gina took a bite and chewed slowly.

"It's delicious. Will you eat with me?"

Sean slid into the chair across from her after grabbing a plate and cup of coffee for himself.

"Where are you headed so early?" Sean asked.

"Church."

"Mind if I join you?"

"I'd like that…very much," she admitted.

"How much time do I have?"

"Thirty minutes."

"Good, I'll be ready in fifteen," he promised.

Sean shoved a mouthful of food into his mouth and dashed off to the bathroom for a shower. As promised, Sean was ready to leave with Gina fifteen minutes later.

Sean hailed a taxi to drop them off at the church they had attended before. Once in the cab, Gina leaned against Sean, still fighting doubts he'd come back because of his love for her. He grasped and caressed her hand gently until the taxi pulled up to the curb.

Once settled into the pew, Sean reached over to hold onto Gina's hand. Gina squeezed his hand in return.

"I'm so glad you came back. I was lost without you," she whispered.

"I'm here to stay," he promised while gazing into her eyes.

"Please don't make promises you can't keep."

"I wouldn't, not in here."

Gina stared briefly into Sean's gentle eyes before returning her attention to the sermon. She hoped so much he *would* stay with her, but he still loved Cindy.

And why would he stay with her if that love for Cindy was strong enough to lure him away? She held firmly onto his hand, praying his return was not a cosmic tease.

She still held these thoughts in her mind while they walked out the building and stopped on the sidewalk. Still holding hands, Sean tugged lightly.

"How about we get lunch at that café?" he suggested.

"I'd like that."

"I'll buy."

Gina smiled moments before Sean kissed her. Heaven had come to her.

I hope this never ends.

****

"I'm calling to see if I can have my job back" are words Sean never thought he'd say. He left a perfectly good job to move out to California with no job of his own once he got there. Now, he had no girlfriend and was left to beg for his old job. He would understand if his boss, actually former boss, said "no" considering a mere one week notice.

In addition, he needed an apartment, pretty tough to get one with no job. So, he rode a taxi to the office first thing Monday morning and pleaded, hoping beyond hope. Fortunately, he was one of the best workers with numerous awards for a knack of doing the right amount of research to enable his clients to make the best decisions for their portfolios.

"This is unprecedented, but yes, you may start tomorrow. Next time, I won't be so cordial."

"There won't be a next time, sir. Thanks so much."

With the most difficult item accomplished, Sean called Pete for the second thing he needed.

"Sean, how's sunny California?"

Billiard Buddies

"Actually, Pete, I never left."

"What? I don't get it. Did Cindy's job fall through?"

"No, she's there," Sean replied.

"So, when do you go out there?"

"I don't. I broke up with her."

"Man, why? I thought you loved her," Pete said.

"I did. I still do in a way, but she loves her job more. I can't live like that."

"Have you called Gina? She was really out of sorts when you announced your move."

"She already knows. She's the main reason I decided to stay. I'm in love with her, Pete."

"Wow, I thought...I didn't..."

"You can't tell the guys, all right? I need a little time to work things out with Gina...and Cindy."

There was a pregnant pause before Pete said, "Okay, I'll keep your secret."

"Great, thanks. When can I pick up the keys for my car?"

"Stop by tonight. Oh, right, how will you get to my place?"

"A taxi is a possibility." He didn't want to lie.

"Where are you staying?"

Sean thought briefly if he dared to say. He had promised long ago not to say he had slept over when he drank too much. This was different though.

"At Gina's," Sean began, "but her cousin Gene is there too," he added, hoping that any crazy thoughts Pete entertained would be squelched.

"Oh, wow. I see."

"Tell no one, Pete, please."

"You have my word, but I want to hear the rest of the story. You have no idea how much I've wanted this for you. You'd been so miserable with Cindy."

"You could tell?"

"Dude, all the guys could tell. They'd all be happy for you, but I'll let you tell them…when you're ready."

"All right, I'll stop by tonight. Thanks, man."

"Bye. I got to get back to work."

Sean hung up the phone wondering why it took him so long to realize what everyone else seemed to have known. He sighed and hailed a taxi to head back to his temporary home.

****

Gina entered her apartment hardly able to contain her excitement about greeting Sean after a long day. She turned the key in the lock and shoved open the door. She remained quiet even upon seeing the man she loved.

"No, Cindy, I haven't changed my mind." Sean paced the floor near the window. "What about my suitcase? Good, I'll pick it up when it arrives."

Gina closed the door silently and dropped her keys on the table.
"Cindy…Cindy…yes, I remember how hard it was when you thought you were pregnant. I remember when it turned out to be cancer. I also remember how sorry I felt when there was nothing I could do to soften your pain."

Gina walked toward the kitchen and sat, still staring at Sean.

"Of course I loved you. I never cheated on you, even when you weren't emotionally available. I'm sorry, Cindy. No, I didn't leave you because you don't want kids or didn't let me touch you. I broke up with you because I'm not your first love and I haven't been in months. I'm not happy with you."

Gina forced herself to breath normally.

"Yeah, just send my stuff back. I'll wire money to you tomorrow. Bye, Cindy."

Sean stared out the window for a few minutes before turning to walk toward a panicked Gina. She held her place, waiting to hear what he had to say.

"Hi there," Sean said. He didn't grant her his usual smile.

"Hi."

"You heard everything?"

"Yeah."

"You all right?"

"I don't know. It sounds like you had a special bond with her. I mean...you thought she was pregnant. That must have done something to you...both of you."

"Oh, Gina," he said, squatting near her knees before placing his hand on hers. "I did feel something real. We'd been dating for four months when she asked me to move in with her. Soon afterwards, we thought she was pregnant, and she freaked. She never wanted kids, especially not at the upswing of her career. Cindy wanted an abortion. The thought of her doing that drove me crazy. I couldn't believe I didn't have a say. Then, we found out she had cancer and she totally

withdrew from me. I felt I owed it to her to help her
through her grief."

"And now?"

"And now, I am with the most beautiful woman I've
ever known and I'm absolutely in love with you."

"Does she have any hold on you? I need to know.
I can't handle any more heartbreak."

"No, she doesn't. She might hope she does, but
I'll never go back to her. It's over. She just needs
some convincing. She's always been more
devoted to her job than she was to me. It's taken
me too long to accept that I'd never satisfy her."
His tone remained lovingly gentle.

Gina glanced toward their hands, but Sean lifted
her head by her chin.

"I won't break your heart. My own would break if I
ever did that to you. I love you, Gina."

"I love you too."

His kiss, so tender, swept her fears and
uncertainty away. She smiled at him in response
to his ever enchanting grin. Without warning, a
serious intensity replaced Sean's grin and he
stood, pulling Gina up out of the chair. He
wrapped his arms around her, one hand on her
lower back, the other a few inches higher, and
kissed her again. The length and eagerness of the
kiss brought Gina to the brink of reconsidering her

decision to wait. Just when she thought she'd lost all reason, Sean stopped and eased away. He had convinced her of his devotion to her.

"Let's go out tonight," he said finally.

"I'd like that."

****

After returning from dinner and a walk in Central Park with Gina, Sean bounded up the stairs toward Pete's apartment. Pete swung open the door in response to him ringing the doorbell.

"It's great to see you, man. I never thought I'd see you this soon," Pete said with a wide grin, his Irish accent bleeding through.

"I know, right?"

"I'm glad you stayed though. So tell me everything."

"I'll tell you everything except the parts I promised not to," Sean corrected.

"Fair enough. You've always been a man of integrity."

"I try, but sometimes I mess up. Anyway…"

Sean explained his feelings for Gina and how they began. He summarized the times when Cindy's job took precedence and the way Gina had been an emotional support although he fought any urges to take their relationship beyond friendship.

"It was tough, you know, having a woman be such a close pal. She knew some of my secrets, even things I hadn't told a guy. I wanted so many times to talk to her about Cindy, but I realized that would've immediately destroyed my connection to Cindy and I really wanted us to work."

"And now?" Pete asked.

"Now, I know that Cindy is not good for me. I would have been such a depressed husband if she'd ever gotten around to saying 'yes'. I'm so glad she put me off. I see now marrying her would have been a huge mistake," Sean explained.

"What about Gina? Do you think she's the one?"

"I know I don't want to live without her. I know she fills my heart with happiness and I totally hate the fact I have to find a place of my own."

"Yeah, about that. How'd you manage to get into her apartment? She'd never let me as much as peek in. Are you two…?"

"Oh, Pete, you know I don't like talking about that."

"I know, but give me something."

"All right. Gene is, in effect, her chaperone. I've been a perfect gentleman and I'd like to keep it that way. That's the only reason she lets me stay."

"Wow, you're amazing, Sean." Pete paused and shook his head. "Yeah, you're…crazy. I don't think I could've done that." He tapped Sean lightly on the shoulder. "So, have you found something?"

"No. I figured I would start searching tomorrow."

"What about the place downstairs…on the first floor? A couple just moved out today. Actually, they got thrown out…couldn't pay the rent."

"Oh, I didn't hear about that. Thanks. I'll talk to the landlord tomorrow. That'll be great. I didn't want to move too far away. I feel I need to catch up on knowing Gina better." Sean glanced at the clock on his cell phone. "I'm gonna go. Gene should be home by now. Do you have my car keys?"

"Yeah," Pete said, strolling over to the kitchen counter. "Here they are."

"Thanks, man." Sean placed his hand on the doorknob. "And to answer your question, I really believe Gina is the one, Pete. I just need to totally close things with Cindy before I can move on. Once I get all my stuff, I won't want to wait long before making my move with Gina. You can't tell anyone though, all right?"

"You got it, Sean. I really respect you. I'll keep your secret."

"Thanks. See you around."

"All right, man. Bye. Tell Gina 'hi' for me."

"I will."

Sean opened the door and saluted Pete before heading down the stairs to return to Gina and, of course, her entertaining cousin Gene.

****

Tuesday brought Sean great success. The landlord gratefully handed over the keys to the apartment on the first floor after Sean paid for the rest of the month and the equivalent of two months' rent to finish out the lease of the previous tenants. Sean couldn't wait to tell Gina his good fortune. After checking out his new pad, Sean rushed upstairs and unlocked the door.

"Hey, Gina! I got an apartment!"

"You're moving out? I thought you would stay a bit longer," she said, sounding disappointed.

"I've gotta do this if I'm to keep my promise to you."

"But you've been great, and I enjoy having you here."

"I love being here with you too, but it takes a lot of self-control not to ravish you." Sean grinned at the sight of Gina's reddening cheeks. "I've been physically attracted to you some time before I'd realized I'd fallen in love with you. That attraction heightened whenever we danced or I stayed over. That's why I returned your key. I didn't know how long I could avoid kissing you or touching you."

"You felt something then too? I thought it was just me," Gina commented.

Man, I wish I knew. If only… No, it's better Cindy and I ended the way we did. Sean smiled and shook his head. "It's also not fair to Gene. He misses hanging out with his friend."

"Did he tell you this?"

"No, but I overheard one of his conversations. You run a tight ship, but he'll do anything for you. He can't be your chaperone indefinitely."

Gina ran her index finger along his forearm. "I suppose you're right. I've been overbearing and mean."

"Not quite so mean. He still loves you," Sean jabbed, and Gina slapped his wrist. Before she had a chance to run off, Sean wrapped his arms around her, pulling her close. "And you can visit me whenever you wish. I'll be downstairs, so we can still see each other every day."

Gina's face brightened, and Sean kissed her on the cheek before she turned to face him.

"How did you manage that?" she asked, her mouth closing in on his.

"Pete. He's pretty resourceful."

"I'll have to remember to thank him," she said before planting one on his lips.

Chapter Thirteen

Not having anything but his bags and the suitcase he picked up at the airport, Sean moved into his new place. His first main purchases, a sofa, a bed, and dining set, did little to fill out the apartment, but at least they made his place a bit more functional. He wasted no time in inviting Gina over for a lamb roast dinner. Gene had been invited too, but he had other plans.

"I like what you did with the place. I brought a bottle of wine to celebrate," Gina said.

"Cool. I think we should stick to one glass with dinner," he suggested, showing her the way to an empty chair. He adjusted the chair once Gina had been seated.

After lighting the candle in the center of the dining table and pouring the wine, Sean sat across from Gina. He held the platters of food so she could choose how much she wished to eat. Once the food was served, Sean said a prayer of thanks for dinner and the special woman with whom he shared the meal.

Gina took a bite, and her eyes sparkled.

"Gosh, Sean, this is really delicious. Gene is going to regret missing this."

"I doubt it. You've finally set him free. I'm sure he's having a blast wherever he is."

She ate another forkful. "You're probably right. It's been a while since you and I had a meal at home...alone. I do enjoy them."

"I thought we could watch a movie after we're finished, if you like."

"That sounds great."

With dinner over and the dishes put away, Gina snuggled into Sean's arms on his new sofa. He kissed her hair often to remind her how much he treasured the moments they shared. During the credits, Sean caressed her cheeks seconds before brushing his lips against hers.

"Which Colbie song would describe this moment?" Sean asked.

"Hmmm. 'You Got Me'. Yeah, I think that song just about sums it up."

"I think I remember that one. Yep, that fits us just fine. I love you so much," Sean said and kissed her again, this time longer than he expected. He didn't want to break away from the euphoria he experienced from moving his lips against hers.

Gina pushed him away.

"It's time I go," she said.

"Stay," he whispered, not wanting to stop just yet. "Sleep over tonight. I won't touch you."

"I can't, Sean."

"You can have the bedroom," he suggested, sneaking a peck on her lips.

"Doesn't seem fair. Why shouldn't I sleep on your sofa as you did on mine?"

He paused long enough to look at her and smirk. "Because then you'd have no way to lock me out." He kissed her neck and added, "Please stay."

"Mmm. Tempting," she said, her voice quivering slightly.

"Good," he replied, rubbing his nose near her temple.

"I think your ten month sabbatical has made you a bit too eager."

"Perhaps." Sean laughed. "You weren't supposed to know about that. I still can't believe I told you."

"I gotta go."

Gina pulled away and headed to the door.

"May I walk you home?" he asked without turning around to face her. He knew, as independent natured as she was, she would want to choose. He didn't want to push his luck.

"Just to the door," she warned.

"Agreed," he said, smiling.

Sean stood, sauntered to the door, and took her hand in his. Gina led the way to her apartment. Before he let her go, he kissed her one last time with a little more enthusiasm.

"Why won't you stay with me tonight?"

Gina shook her head. "Because I don't trust myself to keep the door locked. Your kisses...they bring me to my breaking point...make me weak."

Sean stroked her cheek with the backside of his fingers. He took a step back.

"That's not my intention. I just want you to know beyond a doubt that I am totally devoted to you...that you're the one I want."

Gina rested her palm against his cheek.

"I am convinced. I am *so* convinced. I love you with all my heart and I can feel your love in the way you hold and kiss me. My doubts are gone."

Sean smiled. Her words made his heart soar. He embraced her one last time before saying "good night" and stood outside her door until he heard the bolt click.

I've got to marry her soon.

Sean scratched his head thoughtfully before heading back to his apartment.

****

Sean knocked on Gina's door. He smiled, recalling all the times he did so while not quite so sober. When she opened the door, her radiant face coaxed a huge grin.

"Hi," he said, leaning against the frame.

"Hello." Gina gestured for him to enter.

"Would you like to join me for the afternoon?" He kissed her on the cheek and headed right into the kitchen, settling into one of the chairs.

"Sure. What did you have in mind?" She closed the door and stepped within inches of his stretched out legs, reaching out to rest her hand into his waiting palm.

"Hmm. Well, we've already done the aquarium, a ball game, museums…"

"Don't forget movies at Pete's," she added with a smirk.

Sean chuckled. "Yeah. That was…something."

"How did you ever survive all those nights at his place?" she teased.

"I'm not sure. Probably why I ended up here, the perfect place to recover." He crossed his ankles and took in her sparkling eyes and full lips. "So, I thought we could go to Grounds for Sculpture in Hamilton."

"In New Jersey? Why there?"

"Well, you like country scenes," he nodded toward a painting on the wall, "and I like getting away from the city once in a while. Have you ever been there?"

"No."

"Good, then we can make fresh memories there together. I'll drive."

Sean intertwined his fingers with Gina's as they walked through the garden dotted with many statues. They stopped at a few for pictures before sitting next to a bubbling brook to study a pile of rocks. He wrapped his arms around Gina when she leaned against his chest.

"What do you think?" he asked.

"Reminds me of a giant. You?"

"A fortress."

Gina nodded. "Yes, I like that." She shifted to the side and peered up into his face. "Thanks for bringing me here. I needed this."

"Me too. I want you to know you can relax around me. We can always come here to take a break from ruthless competition."

Gina giggled. "This isn't all a ploy to get me to lower my defenses, is it?"

"Nope. Of course not," he said with a wink.

She giggled again. "Good." She snuggled back into his arms. "I needed this…with you. I'd like to come back. I love you, Sean."

Sean kissed her forehead. "I love you too."

Sean would long remember the first time he and Gina showed up together at the bar holding hands. He thought he'd have to scrape the jaw of every guy off the floor. Pete did a great job keeping his newfound relationship with Gina a secret. Once he explained enough to satisfy his friends' curiosity, the guys all patted him on the back for good luck.

Love did not lessen the fury with which Gina played the game. He could not let up for one moment thinking he would have an easy win. In fact, he worked even harder for the one match with which he walked away. Still, the championship evaded them both.

However, even as he studied Gina's intense expression before she took her next shot, he thought about the need to close the door on his life with Cindy once and for all. Having received the last of his possessions back from California, Sean called Cindy for a final word.

"Hi, Sean. I miss you," Cindy said the second she answered the phone.

"I got everything. Thanks for sending the boxes," he said without addressing her comment. "Do you need more money?"

"No, it was more than enough. In fact, I have a surplus I can mail to you."

"No, don't worry about that. Keep it. You all settled?"

"Yes, and the job's going really well. I'm working like a horse, but I like being busy."

"Yeah, busy suits you," Sean agreed.

"What about you? Did you get your job back? You never said."

"Yes. My boss gave me a tongue-lashing, but I'm back. It's been good."

"And Gina. Are you still seeing her?"

"Yes, in fact, our relationship is progressing very well."

"Are you going to marry her?"

"That's likely, yes."

"Oh," Cindy exhaled audibly.

"So, this will be the last time I call, and I would appreciate if you didn't call me anymore."

"Sean, please. I need you in my life. I want you in my life."

"We were over, Cindy, long before you decided to move out West. After three weeks of mulling over our relationship, I realize that although I care about you, I don't love you romantically anymore. That ship has sailed."

Cindy sniffled. Sean could tell she started crying.

"I'm so sorry, Sean. I never meant to hurt you. You were supposed to be the one for me. I messed up. I still love you. Is there anything I could do to change your mind?"

"No. This is good-bye."

"Okay. That's it then. I chose a demanding career and lost you."

"You chose your career instead of me. It just took me a while to realize that."

Cindy blew her nose and coughed.

"You'll be successful at what you do. I know you will. I wish you the best in your life. Take care of yourself," Sean said without any emotional attachment. He knew without a doubt his feelings for her had died as well.

"I wish you the same, Sean. Stay safe. Bye."

"Bye," he said and hung up the phone.

Sean stared at his cell for a few minutes and began pushing buttons. Upon finding Cindy's name in the address book, Sean pressed the delete button. Now, he had declared to himself that Cindy was in the past. The time had come for him to move on.

Sean immediately rushed upstairs to talk to Gina. He didn't want to waste any time telling her he was finally ready to take the next step. He grinned upon seeing her beautiful smiling face. *I feel like I'm in high school doing this.*

"Gina, will you be my girlfriend?"

Gina blinked and covered her mouth with her hands. "Is this for real? You're ready?"

"Yeah. I erased Cindy from my phone. I don't feel anything for her anymore. I know I'm ready to move on with you by my side."

"Then, yes, Sean, I will be happy to be your girlfriend."

Sean grabbed Gina, lifting her off her feet. He turned around and kissed her as he slowly returned her to the floor.

"You have made me so happy. Thanks for being in my life," Sean said before he hugged Gina tightly.

****

A few days later, Sean surprised Gina with an outing at a theatrical production on Broadway to celebrate the new turn their relationship had taken. Sean had never seen Gina so thrilled. He hardly remembered a time when she hadn't been around.

"The day your apartment flooded, why did you cry?" he asked after they exited the building.

"You didn't belong to me. I couldn't be yours."

"Things were so crazy and you were so sad, I almost kissed you," he confessed.

"I probably wouldn't have stopped you, but I would have regretted it later."

"Do you feel regret now?"

Gina shook her head. "No. No regrets. I love you."

"I love you," he echoed and gently palmed her cheeks before pressing his lips to hers.

Upon arriving at Gina's apartment, Sean kissed her good-night. However, Gina's cell phone rang before he walked away. She stared at the caller id and all the color drained from her face.

"It's Hank," she gasped, her once sparkling eyes now expressing despair.

"May I have the phone?" Sean asked. Gina looked puzzled. "*I'll* talk to Hank. You shouldn't have to deal with him anymore."

Gina handed the phone to Sean. Sean placed the phone against his ear.

"Hey there, Hank," Sean said.

"Who, who is this? Where's Gina?" Hank asked, his tone tense.

"Oh, she's right here, but she doesn't want to talk to you. As for me, well, we haven't officially met, so let me introduce myself. My name is Sean Savage, Gina's boyfriend."

"You! She pretended you didn't exist. Yet here you are."

"She never lied to you, Hank. We've been just friends until recently. However, now that things are serious between us, I'd appreciate your not calling or coming around anymore."

"Just like that you expect me to just stay away. Well, you tell her that until she's hitched, I'm not giving up."

Sean heard a click.

"Sean? What happened? What did he say?" Gina asked, clearly concerned.

"He's going to be a problem. I'd suggest not answering the phone when he calls, but it's up to you. He's not giving you up without a fight. I'll be sure to give him one. I don't scare easy."

"Please be careful. I don't know what he'll do, and I will lose my mind if you're hurt," Gina begged.

"I will. You too, okay?"

"Yes," she replied and buried her head into his neck.

Chapter Fourteen

Sean called Gene a few days later, nerves threatening his typically calm demeanor. However, he dared not wait any longer and Gene knew Gina best.

"Hi, Sean," Gene answered. "This is a surprise."

"Hey, Gene. Would you meet me on Fifth Avenue on the corner of Fifty-Second Street today at noon?"

"Where are we going?"

"You'll know when you get there. Meet me inside."

"Sure, I'll be there," Gene promised.

Sean strolled along the many glass-covered showcases. Stones of every color sparkled. They all seemed to call out to him, "Pick me. I'm the perfect one for her."

"So, I think I know why you're here. But why did you ask me to come?"

Sean smiled and turned to Gene. So many thoughts flashed through his mind that he didn't even notice Gene strutting up behind him.

"You knew this was coming, didn't you? You didn't even call to find out where I was."

"Well, yes, I knew you were crazy about Gina. She's crazy about you too."

"Is she crazy enough to marry a guy she hasn't even known for a year? That's why I asked you to come. Do you think it's too soon to ask for her hand in marriage?"

Gene grinned and glanced toward the rings on display.

"No way. She was ready when you came back for her. We've been waiting for you to get around to asking her."

Sean's arm hairs stood on end. He couldn't believe what he heard. He wondered how he could have been so clueless as to her intense feelings for him.

"Wow! Would you help me pick one that's perfect for her? I'd like to ask her tomorrow when I take her to Central Park. It has to be our secret though."

Gene raised his right hand and said, "I swear to not let my favorite cousin in on this little secret no matter how excited I get choosing her engagement ring." Gene lowered his arm. "So, what catches your eye?"

"There's this one I really like. Come, I'll show you," Sean said, heart pumping faster.

Sean rushed to the other side of the store where the display case held the ring he favored. He became ecstatic when Gene covered his mouth with his hands.

"She'll really love this one," Gene said, wiping a tear from his cheek. "You already know her. I'm glad you came into her life. I can't remember her ever being happier. Thanks, Sean."

"She saved me from an empty love life. I can't imagine my life without her. Thanks for coming, Gene. You're the best."

"I believe you can handle the rest on your own. Be sure to call me once you've asked her. I want to hear her squeals."

"I will."

Gene gave Sean a quick hug before strutting out of the store, the same way he always did.

****

Gina lay on a blanket under a flowering tree in Central Park. Her skin tingled every time Sean touched her. It seemed like a dream, and yet it wasn't, for he had come back to her. With each kiss, she wished to be alone with him, something she knew she dared not do...at least not yet. She giggled whenever he tickled her. She couldn't remember ever being this happy.

Sean continued to kiss Gina gently, each touch creating a new memory, a new sensation. Again, she wished to be alone with him…indoors. She half-expected a passer-by to yell "Get a room," but no one did. She turned her head away slightly to halt his advances before yielding to the purple haze of passion.

Heeding to her wishes, he gazed at her dreamily before resting his forehead onto the side of her neck. He breathed slowly while his hand reached for his pocket. He moved his pocketed hand around as if searching for something.

She shook her head quickly trying to rid the sensual thoughts running through her mind. *I can't,* she thought. *I must wait for that elusive "I do" before I give myself like that to someone…again.* She sat up and stared across the park.

"Are you all right?" he asked, rising to sit on his heels, only one hand visible, palm down on the grass to one side.

She looked at him and touched his olive-toned cheek.

"Do you miss her?"

Seemingly startled at her question, he replied, "No. I'm over her. You're the only one in my heart, in my mind. I love you and only you."

"I'm afraid. I just want to make sure you're really mine."

"I am. I promise."

She smiled.

****

Sean studied Gina's sweet face while the wind whipped blond curls across her chin. He wondered if he would ever calm her fears about his relationship with Cindy. Gina had become the only woman with whom he yearned to spend a lifetime.

Slowly, he removed his hand from his pocket where he had fingered the ring. He would not ask her here. The time was not quite right, and the place, well, the place needed to be memorable, more memorable than a park under blue cloudless skies.
"Would you like to go out to dinner tonight? I have someplace special in mind."

"Of course."

"Feel free to dress up. It's sort of a fancy place. I'll stop by your place at six."

Sean stood and extended his arms so he could help Gina up. He wrapped Gina in his arms and kissed her once more before taking her hand so they could head toward the nearest park exit. He only had a few hours to make reservations at the perfect location, Spirit of New York.

Fortunately, Sean landed a reservation for two. Normally, pulling off such a feat a few hours before dinner would prove unlikely, but Sean learned that he lucked out. Another couple had just cancelled.

Sean ordered purple Tulips for the dinner table's centerpiece and requested special music to be played throughout the evening. He even included a couple Colbie Caillat tunes. Dressed in a white shirt with purple tie and black slacks, Sean hoped to stir Gina's senses in anticipation of something amazing.

Gina opened her door in answer to his knock and the sight of her nearly took his breath away. Of course, she wore a form fitted halter-top dress splattered with purple patterns.

"Wow! You look great, Gina."

"Thanks. I like your tie," she said, smiling.

"I thought you would. Shall we go then?"

"Yes," Gina replied, locking her door seconds before taking Sean's arm.

Sean helped Gina into the taxi he requested. He decided it was better to plan ahead just in case. A cab would also be waiting for them when the boat pulled into harbor. With those details covered,

Sean could focus on the most important event of the evening—asking Gina to be his wife.

****

Gina's eyes sparkled when she spotted the tulips at the table Sean reserved for their evening together. They chatted over dinner with Gina expressing how she was enjoying her first time on the Spirit of New York. Sean relaxed slightly just knowing Gina was having a blast.

Once they had finished dessert, Sean took Gina out on the deck to take in the sights under a mid-Spring evening sky. He held her close while she stared at the New York City sky-line. The wind whipped at Gina's curls which she pushed behind an ear with a gentle swipe. His heart beat a bit faster. He wanted to kiss her now and not stop. After a few minutes, he turned Gina so he could gaze into her dazzling eyes. He knew the breeze tussled his hair, but he didn't care.

"I've been nervous all day about dinner tonight," Sean said, shifting uneasily. "The last time I tried hooking you up with a guy, you became rather abrasive."

She smiled slyly as if remembering her outburst against him that fateful night some time ago.

"But I'm willing to take another shot since that guy is now me," he continued.

Sean pulled out a box and placed it on his palm. Gina's jaw dropped and eyes widened as he opened the box. Upon seeing the ring, Gina clasped her hands over her mouth and tears began to form in her eyes.

"I want you in my life for the rest of my life. I want to wake up every day with you in my arms and take care of you. I want to make babies with you and dance," he admitted.

Gina touched the ring and then stared lovingly at Sean.

"I know we've only been dating for four weeks, but will you marry me?" Sean asked. "I love you and I promise you won't have to suffer through Colbie's more somber songs as long as I'm alive."

He got down on one knee and grabbed the ring, endowed with a solitaire diamond surrounded by Amethyst gems set in white gold. He placed the box into a pocket and waited until Gina caught her breath.

"Yes," she gasped. "I will. We may have only been dating for four weeks, but we've known each other for much longer. You've grown on me." She paused to caress his cheek. "It's why I had such a hard time letting you go. I want this. I want you. My heart is yours."

"Great," he said, sliding the ring onto her finger. "There's more."

Gina gazed intently at Sean while he stood up before her.

"What is it?" she asked, furrowing her eyebrows slightly.

"I don't want to wait a year or even a month. I would marry you tomorrow if I could. What I'm trying to say is I want you to be my wife as soon as possible. Are you game?"

Gina nodded excitedly with a huge grin. "You have no idea how much I wanted you to say that. I was afraid you would want to wait," she confessed.

"No way. I've been trying to get married for a while now. I know now it didn't happen because I was pursuing the wrong person. So, can we start planning tomorrow?"

"Yes, let's do this," she agreed.

Sean grinned and pulled Gina toward him, pressing his lips against hers. Her warmth flowed through him, and he seemed to float miles above where they stood.

"I love you so much, Gina. Thank you for agreeing to spend the rest of your life with me."

"I love you too. Thanks for making this night a moment I will never ever forget."

****

Sean and Gina spent the next few days calling churches for available dates and visiting the Marriage Bureau at the City Clerk's Office to obtain a marriage license. Once the date was set for them to marry at the church they had attended in secret before Cindy moved away, Sean secured a room in a restaurant for the wedding reception.

Sean and his future wife were sitting quietly on a bench in Central Park when Gina's phone rang. Gina stared at her phone and sighed.

"Hank?" Sean asked.

"Yeah," she said, quietly. "I thought we were past this."

"You want to talk to him or do you want me to?"

"I'll talk to him."

Gina reluctantly answered the phone.

"Hi, Hank. I thought you understood that there's no hope for us." She paused, listening. "No, we've *been* through. You keep trying to get back together, but there's no chance of that, not now, not ever." Gina paused again. "Yes, he's here with me, but I'd be telling you the same thing even if he wasn't. Why don't you just leave me alone? My life is with Sean now."

At that statement, Sean offered his hand, palm up.

Billiard Buddies

"Let me try?"

Gina nodded and quickly handed Sean her cell.

"Hey, Hank."

"Why does she *do* that? Why did she hand you the phone? I wasn't finished talking to her," Hank growled.

"You *are* done talking to Gina, Hank. You see, Gina is my fiancée. We'll be married in a few days, so I would appreciate you not calling her anymore. She no longer needs you to look in on her."

"Gina's marrying *you*? But you haven't known her that long," Hank said, this time quietly.

"Do I have your word that you'll leave her alone?"

Sean heard Hank sigh heavily on the other end.

"Yeah. I won't call anymore."

"Or come around. You'd have to face me first," Sean warned.

"Don't worry man. I'm done. Tell her."

"I will. Bye, Hank."

Sean pressed the end call button and handed the phone back to Gina. She stared at him with searching eyes.

"Well? What did he say? Will he stop?" she asked.

"I believe you won't be hearing from him anymore."

"Thanks, Sean."

"After the first time I played against you, I never thought you'd need my help with anything. You've always displayed a tough exterior."

"I'm not so tough."

"Neither am I," he said before leaning toward her for a kiss.

****

Sean and Gina shared their happy news with the guys at the next pool night in their usual bar. Everyone clanked beer bottles in celebration of a union between the best pool players they knew. Sean began strolling to the bar to order another round when he noticed Cindy standing in the entrance. He quickly glanced back at Gina who by now had also noticed Cindy's arrival. His heart fell, not because Cindy appeared, but because Gina's eyes were filled with dismay.

What is she doing here? Of all the times she decides to see where I play, it had to be now.

Sean returned to Gina and stood in front of her, hoping to block her view of Cindy.

"Gina, look at me," he said.

"What?" Gina responded, straining to look passed him.

"It's you I love."

She peered up into his eyes.

"I know," she said sadly.

"We are getting married in two days. I promise."

"I believe you. I trust you."

Sean stepped briskly toward Cindy who stood motionless, clutching a silver purse with both hands.

"I couldn't find you, so I came here," Cindy began. "I've been checking for days now. I couldn't remember when you played pool with the guys...and with Gina."

"Where are you staying?" Sean asked, ignoring her prattle.

"At the Grand Hyatt, downtown."

"Let's go. I'll follow you. I don't want to go into this conversation here."

Cindy nodded and led the way out.

When they arrived in the lobby of her hotel, Sean directed Cindy to a lounge area. He sat and glowered at her.

"Why are you here?" Sean asked, perturbed.

"I've been calling for weeks, but you never answer your phone. I became both worried and scared. Worried because I thought something had happened to you and scared that you just didn't want to speak to me. I guess it's the latter." She looked down at her hands.

"I'm getting married in two days," Sean offered, not caring how abrupt he seemed to Cindy. As far as he was concerned, he had broken things off with her. His previous phone call had made that clear.

"What? But that's so soon."

"She's my one. I saw no reason to wait."

"She stole you from me. You were mine," Cindy objected, her face turning bright red.

Sean huffed through his nose.

"Gina did not steal me away. She fought hard not to. So much so, I didn't even know she had fallen in love with me. You were the one who opened my eyes. I left you because you are too doggone selfish."

"Why? Because I couldn't have sex with you?"
she said, straightening her spine in a haughty
fashion.

"No way. If that were the case, I'd have left
months ago. You were selfish with your time, your
affection, and with you. I had a tough time
bonding with you when you were never around."

"Sure. I bet Gina is giving you some."

Sean thought better of sharing personal details
about Gina with Cindy. However, he figured it was
more risky not to.

"I've never made love to Gina. We're waiting until
after we marry. We've connected because we're
invested into each other. I am totally in love with
her and can't see my future without her."

Sean could tell Cindy had become perplexed
because she began wringing her hands.

"I thought you two…I didn't know what I had. Now,
I've lost you," she gasped before tears streamed
down her face.

Sean sat staring at Cindy for a few minutes before
offering her a comforting embrace.

"You must hate me," Cindy sniffled.

"I don't, but I no longer love you like I did. You're
lumped into a bucket with the rest of humanity. I
care that you're safe. Nothing more."

"I'm so sorry. I didn't mean to hurt you. I took you for granted. I've lost a good man."

"I forgive you," Sean said.

"Thanks."

Sean released Cindy and eased away.

"You can't come around anymore. I'm starting over and I don't want you upsetting Gina."

"I know. I'm a bit too possessive to be allowed the pleasure of visiting you. I do ask a favor, though."

"What is it?"

"May I come to your wedding? It'll help me close the door on us."

Sean became stern. He didn't want to hurt her, but he wanted less to harm his new bride.

She'd never let up if I refuse her request. How am I going to explain this to Gina? Sean sighed, unable to think of another solution. "You may attend the wedding, but don't you dare mess things up for me. I don't know that I could forgive you for that."

Cindy nodded.

****

Billiard Buddies

Gina told the guys "good night" thirty minutes after Sean left with Cindy. She did not want to spend the next hour or more playing pool while her future with Sean remained uncertain. Sure, she trusted he would make the best decision, but she wondered if that decision meant she would remain a part of his life now that Cindy had appeared in the flesh.

She closed her door and leaned against it while turning the lock. After a few minutes, she walked to the kitchen and filled a glass with water. She sipped sparingly, staring at the cabinet in front of her. Soon afterwards, she headed for the sofa.

At least these have been the best days ever, she thought, already dreading the worst. Sean, as loyal as they come, may choose to return to Cindy. The emotional history he shared with his ex would surely tug at his heart. *How could anyone blame him for being caught up in a whirlwind romance?*

Gina heard the door latch click, not sure how much time had passed since she sat on her sofa, holding her cell, waiting for Sean to call. His form filled the doorway, and she stood, stepping lightly toward him. She dared not speak for the tears would surely come. He tilted his head, staring at her with gentle eyes.

Here it comes.

But, he spread his arms apart inviting an embrace. She rushed between his arms and nestled against his chest.

"It's over," Sean said.

"Us?" she asked, hoping not, but expecting it nonetheless.

"No, silly. Cindy and I are over. We have been, but I think she finally sees it now. I thought you were clear on that," he said and kissed her head.

"I was. I am. It's just that this, us, is like a fairy tale I keep dreading I'll wake up from."

"Then I'd be screaming 'cause I love this life with you even if it's a dream. I don't want to wake up." Sean lifted her up into his arms and carried her to the sofa.

He plopped down and placed her legs across his lap. "There's one glitch."

"What's that?" Gina asked, wondering what could ever affect her now that she knew Sean remained drawn to her.

"She's coming to the wedding."

Gina gasped.

"She won't cause a scene. At least, she better not. She'll leave us alone after she sees it happen. You'll see."

*I have to trust him. He'd never let her come if
there was another way to get her to stay away.*
"Okay. I won't like it, but if that helps her to leave
us alone, then I'll allow it."

Sean cupped her face and kissed her
enthusiastically. Gina could hardly wait for an
unlimited supply of such intimacy. Sean
reluctantly stopped kissing her.

"Two days seem much too far away. I gotta go,"
Sean said. He gently pushed her legs off his and
stood.

"I thought guys like you no longer existed," Gina
said, impressed by Sean's self-control. She never
worried about Sean's advances. He always knew
when to stop.

"We're out there. We just don't know we can be
that way. I guess we just need the right woman to
come along and unlock that possibility." Sean
smiled and stepped backwards toward the door.
"See you at rehearsal tomorrow," he said before
blowing her a kiss.

After he left, Gina lay on the sofa hugging a pillow
and thinking about all the times he'd never have to
leave when he said "good night".

Chapter Fifteen

"I can't believe you asked me to give you away," Gene said while fussing with Gina's hair.

"It looks fine, Cous'," she said, brushing his hand away. "Who else was I gonna ask? You're the last male relative in our family line." Gina paused to study her cousin's beautifully feminine features. "And I love you more than life and want you to be a part of the best time of my life. You've made me laugh when I felt like crying. You're the best girlfriend I ever had." With those words, Gina kissed him on his now damp cheek.

"Joanna wouldn't be pleased." Gene hugged Gina loosely.

"She's my bridesmaid. She'd understand."

"I'm going to be a mess before we even reach the altar," Gene admitted while briskly fanning his face. "I'm proud to do this for you. Now let's go before your groom wonders where you are."

Gene helped Gina into the limo before climbing in beside her. The ride to the church seemed to go quickly. Gene entered the church to check whether Sean had already arrived. Gina stared intently at the entrance until he returned.

"Sean's ready, sweetie. Don't keep him waiting any longer."

Gina gave Gene her hand and carefully stepped out of the car.

"You're beautiful, Gina, just like your mom. She and your dad would have been so proud of you today."

"I know, Gene. On a day like today, I miss them very much." Gina breathed deeply. "I'm ready. Let's go get me married."

Gene smiled at Gina when she hooked his arm. They walked through the entrance and down the aisle to the man of her dreams.

****

"Pete, help me with my tie. She'll be here soon," Sean said anxiously.

"Calm down. Your best man won't see you looking a mess to meet your bride."

Pete straightened Sean's tie and grinned. "She's sure to have trouble controlling herself tonight. You look great."

Sean chuckled.

"Cut it out, Pete." Sean checked his overall appearance before finally turning away from the mirror. "I don't know why I'm so worried about how I look. She's seen me in a not-quite-so-dashing state."

Sean noticed Pete's raised eyebrow, but Sean ignored his friend's silent question.

"Pete, thanks for everything, especially getting me to meet Gina. I thought I had everything. I thought I was okay. Now, I can hardly remember what it feels like without her. I am so ready for this."

"Glad I could help. We guys knew for a long while that Gina needed someone special. You're the only one special enough to give her what she really needs. You are loyal and trustworthy. And you play a mean game of pool. I don't think she could ever be happy with someone she could consistently beat."

Sean turned to see Gene's head stuck through the partially open door.

"Are you ready for your girl?" Gene asked.

"You bet," Sean answered. "I'll tell the minister we're ready." Gene nodded and began backing up. "Hey, Gene?"

"Yeah, darlin'?"

"Thanks for being such a good friend. You made me nervous when I first met you, but you're a really cool person. I look forward to getting to know you better."

"Same here. Now, let me go so I can bring her to you. You look like you're about to burst," Gene jeered and quickly strutted away in his Armani suit.

Sean smiled to himself.

"C'mon, Sean, the minister's waiting. You're on," Pete said, ushering Sean toward the open door.

"Great. Let's go."

Sean found it difficult to stand in place while Gina gradually made her way toward him to the song "Tailor Made". He'd often thought that Gina fit him like a tailor made glove, so the lyrics in this song seemed apropos.

He realized he began grinning without even trying in response to her great smile and the way Gina's white dress accentuated her curves. Sean graciously accepted Gina's hand from Gene. The vows he shared with Gina seemed to pale in comparison to the way his heart thumped at being linked to hers.

****

When Cindy arrived during the ceremony, Gina shivered and her hands felt clammy. However, when Sean caressed her hands, Gina turned her head to dote on him instead.

"She doesn't matter, not today, not ever," Sean assured Gina. "It's just us. She needs to see this to bring resolution for herself. After today, she's out of our lives."

"All right, then I'll only have eyes for you."

Sean flashed a wide grinned which relaxed Gina. She smiled in response to let him know she'd be okay.

"I now pronounce you man and wife."

As soon as the minister finished saying those words, Sean leaned toward Gina, pressing his lips against hers. She felt the warmth of his mouth while he slowly moved his lips. His tongue brushed hers and he pulled her closer still. Gina lost all sense of time, forgetting about Cindy, forgetting fear. She closed her eyes to let the sensations flow through her body. Nothing mattered but this moment when she was his and he hers for a lifetime.

Sean pulled away slowly and leaned his brow against her forehead. He kissed her again and winked.

"Hey, beautiful, we're hitched," Sean said joyfully.

"Thank you for loving me."

Sean shook his head slightly.

"Thank *you* for freeing my heart to feel true love. You are my lifetime mate."

He gave her a quick peck.

"Ready to stop?" he asked.

"No, not at all, but we'd better. Everyone's already cheering. I think I hear Pete howling."

"That's why he's the best man."

Sean took Gina by the hand and ran out the sanctuary under a shower of bubbles. Upon reaching the limo, they scurried inside and began kissing each other intensely. Gina wondered if they would make it to the restaurant still dressed. That mattered little, except for the driver. They were married now.

"Are you sure you don't want to just get a hotel room in town?" Sean asked. "Niagara Falls is almost an eight hour drive."

"No, I can manage the ride," she said quickly.

"I don't think I can."

"Oh?" Gina straightened herself into a fully sitting position, feeling suddenly nervous.

"You seem agitated. What's the matter? Did I do something wrong?"

"No, you've been perfect. It's me and my silly emotions." Gina realized with their relationship taking an accelerated route, there were things she never told Sean and being a perfect gentleman, he never asked.

"Then tell me. You're my wife now and I want to know what bugs you even if I can't fix it. Are you nervous about sleeping with me? Are you…is this your first time?"

"No," she said, shaking her head. "It happened with my first boyfriend, a guy before Hank. At first I thought I wanted to be with him, but then I changed my mind. He didn't want to stop." She exhaled audibly. "He had a bit much to drink. I did too. I started fighting him off, but I lost the fight and let him have me. Even boozed up, it hurt a lot. That experience reinforced why I never wanted Hank to touch me. Friends matched me up with both of them," she explained.

"So, that's why you freaked when I tried to set you up with Greg. I'm so sorry, Gina."

"It's in the past now. I didn't want to until…you're the first guy I wanted that way. That scared me a little at first. Well…actually a lot." Gina sighed. "I look forward to our first time together. I *do* want to be with you."

"So, why are you so nervous?"

"I'm afraid that making love to you will hurt physically. I'm afraid of ruining our first night together. I can't believe I'm messing things up for us today."

Sean reached out to cradle Gina's cheek in his palm. "No, you're not messing things up. I'm glad you told me. I understand so much more about why you kept your distance. You don't have to do that anymore and you don't have to worry about tonight. It'll be fine. I can't wait to be with you, either, but I want you to tell me if I'm hurting you. I'll adjust. I want our time together to be special for both of us. All right?"

Gina nodded. "Okay."

Sean let his hand slide down her arm. He squeezed her hand. "We'll be there soon."

"So we have time for one more kiss?"

"Yeah," Sean whispered and brushed his lips against Gina's.

She responded with urgent kisses.

"You better have Pete call the hotel. We can go to the falls tomorrow," she suggested. Her new husband managed a smothered "okay" under Gina's increasing passion.

Everyone posed for pictures outside the white reception hall with columns ringed with gold paint before entering for a catered meal of steak or chicken and sides. Gina noticed Pete standing aside to make a phone call when her new husband returned to her after a brief conversation with his friend.

Sean spent the reception stealing kisses from Gina to which she joyfully submitted. He knew her deepest secret and still wanted her. She told her worst fears and his understanding dispelled them from her mind and heart. Sean would take care of her when she was most vulnerable. She believed that with all her heart. After two hours of eating and dancing, Gina cheerfully left with Sean for the hotel Pete had called earlier.

****

When they arrived at the room, Gina volunteered to be the first to get ready for bed. Sean thought of joining her, but figured it was best to take it slow. When Gina emerged, she was a vision dressed in a sheer cream nightie covered by a robe of the same material. It took all of Sean's self-control and more he didn't know he had in reserve to head to the bathroom to get cleaned up.

After he reentered the main room, Sean lit the candles and walked toward the bed on which Gina sat. He was topless. It seemed for a moment Gina had forgotten how to breathe.

"With or without?" Sean asked, holding up a condom.

"With." Gina smiled. "I'm not ready to be a mother just yet."

Gently, Sean climbed onto the bed and started kissing Gina with sensual passion. He loved her fully, and she willingly gave herself to him. Each kiss communicated love, and each touch expressed their passion for the other.

As their bodies melded together, Gina jolted a bit. Sean paused and gazed at her eyes. He could tell that she hurt, but her eyes bid him to continue. Sean understood her language now. He had spent much time studying them during happy conversations about plans for the future, or fights over decisions about the wedding. After missing or ignoring the messages so many times prior to his almost departure to California, Sean made it his duty to interpret their meaning expressed in her eyes. Although his body drove him to keep going, his deep love for her made him willing to stop for her. Her kiss on his lips convinced him that he understood perfectly.

This expression of their love for each other culminated in ecstasy for them both. He knew she trusted him with her life and her love. Sean expressed fully the adoration he had for Gina in everything he had done for her, and also now with the tenderness with which he beheld her. Lovemaking expressed all he felt for her, and more.

Sean enfolded Gina in his arms as they fell asleep.

The next morning, when they awoke, Gina and Sean smiled lovingly at each other. She admitted to feeling a bit sore, but other than that she seemed happy to finally be free of the walls she had built to protect herself.

"So, now that we're married, can you tell me the secret recipe?" Sean asked as he stroked her cheek.

Gina smiled and leaned to his ear. She whispered something.

Sean giggled. "Wow, cool."

They kissed again. Niagara Falls would have to wait another day.

****

"You're losing your touch, Sean. Is this what happens when a guy gets married? He lets his woman win?" Pete jeered two weeks later during the revival of the fight toward billiard supremacy.

"I have no intention of *letting* Gina win."

"That's because you know this game is already mine," Gina boasted.

Sean took the shot and missed.

Gina blew on her stick and took the last two shots to win the game.

Sean put the pool stick down and walked over to kiss Gina.

"Hey, love birds. Take it home. There's a bunch of single guys here," Pete said. "To think I said 'I think I've found your match'. I had no idea," he said, smiling.

"C'mon, my love. May I walk you home?" Sean asked.

"Anytime," Gina said.

Sean clasped her hand, waved bye to the guys, and walked down the street.

"You know, I'll beat you tomorrow," Sean promised.

"Maybe, but not without a fight," Gina rebutted.

"There's one place where we can both be winners."

"Where's that?"

"The bedroom."

Gina giggled.

"Is your cousin coming over?"

"No, he's avoiding us—something about us still being busy on our honeymoon."

"He may be avoiding us for a while. I held back for too long. I intend to make up for that."

Sean put his arm around Gina's waist as they walked back to the apartment.

She giggled again.

"Let's go home, wife," Sean suggested.

"Yes, let's...*husband*," Gina agreed.

Off they went to make love blossom in their lives together.

Epilogue

Sean took a shot and the ball banked twice, but only hovered near the left center pocket. He bowed his head in defeat.

Gina smiled and grabbed her glass of ginger ale. She sipped it slowly before placing her drink on a small table.

"One more game for the match," she said. "Want some action?"

"What did you have in mind?" Sean teased.

"Money, silly. A girl needs things."

"Yeah, I know. Sure."

Gina nodded as everyone followed her, each dropping twenty into the winner's basket. Sean racked up the balls and stepped away. She stood for a moment, studying the table, with one hand on a hip with fingers spread across her back, the other holding her special cue. Finally, she stepped forward, leaned over the edge, and pushed hard at the butt.

Success! Two striped balls in the same pocket. She paced around the table with a brief glance toward Sean. *We've sure had some good months together. I hate to do this to him, but not quite enough.* This time, instead of anger, fierce love fueled her game, love for her husband's heart and for the small rapidly beating heart inside her. Gina pressed her enlarged abdomen against a short side of the pool table. *C'mon, kiddo, give Mama a little more leeway. Move.* The baby in her womb kicked—possibly in defiance—before relinquishing its comfy position. *That's it.*

She focused and lined up the end of the cue from an angle. She hoped to down three balls in a kind of domino effect—cue ball clicked two where one sank into the far right pocket and the other clacked a friend down another hole.

Sean sighed audibly. Sweat beaded on his forehead. A drop spread across fibers in his blue shirt. She had this one. The next two shots came easy.

"Ready to forfeit, honey?" Gina jabbed.

"No way. Game's not over yet."

"All right," she said and took the eight ball with finesse. "It's about time the championship returned to its rightful owner."

"Not for long," Sean promised, closing the distance between them.

"You wouldn't try to beat a pregnant lady, would you?"

He smirked, sliding a hand over a bump the baby made with its foot.

Billiard Buddies

"One month 'til birth. Another to recuperate, give or take a few weeks. I'm a very patient man, but you already know this. I'll get the championship again."

"We'll see. Such a shame our baby will have to witness Daddy losing to Mommy first time out."

"No mercy," he whispered, pulling her close.

"Ditto. Happy first Anniversary, love of my life."

"Happy Anniversary."
(Smooch!)

The End.

(Influenced by Colbie Caillat songs: Oxygen and Realize "If you just realize what I just realized.")

Cassandra Ulrich

About the Author

Cassandra Ulrich was born on the beautiful island of St. Croix, United States Virgin Islands, located east of Puerto Rico. Living in the tropics fueled her imagination and day dreams. For years, she wrote poetry and entered competitions. However, only many years later did she discover joy in writing stories longer than a few pages.

She published her first young adult novel, *A Beautiful Girl*, in April 2011. The inspirational novel has already touched many hearts ranging from teens to adults.

Her second novel, *Love's Intensity*, a teen paranormal romance, was released on July 11, 2013.

Her third, *Billiard Buddies*, a New Adult romance novella, was released on May 24, 2014.

On June 25, 2014, she published/released *Real Purpose: You Are Special*, poetry written while in high school and college. She released *Life Experienced* later that summer.

On June 25, 2016, she published/released two more poetical compilations: *Encouraging Through Sharing: A Christian's Perspective* and *A Love Gift*.

I Exist. Hear Me. won first place in the South Jersey Writers' Group 2018 Poetry Contest, short story, *"Adelle and Brandon"* was released on August 29, 2018, short story *Zale's Tale* won a spot in *Beach Fun* released by Cat & Mouse Press in October 2018, and short story Battle at Kitee made it to the semi-finals in the Mad Scientist 2019 Science Fiction Writing contest.

For more information,
Web Page: cassandraulrich.com
Blog Page: cassandraulrich.blogspot.com
Twitter Page: https://twitter.com/CassandraUlric1
FaceBook Page:
https://www.facebook.com/CassandraUlrichAuthor
Goodreads Page:
http://www.goodreads.com/author/show/6925111.Cassandra_Ulric
h
Amazon Author Page: http://amazon.com/author/cassandraulrich
Smashwords Author Page:
http://www.smashwords.com/profile/view/cassandraulrich?ref=cass
andraulrich

CONNECT WITH ME ONLINE

Web: http://cassandraulrich.com/

Facebook Fan Page:
https://www.facebook.com/CassandraUlrichAuthor

Facebook Group:
https://www.facebook.com/groups/cassandraulrich
journey/

My Blog: http://cassandraulrich.blogspot.com/

Twitter: @CassandraUlric1

Made in the USA
Middletown, DE
11 October 2020